SAY MY NAME

SAY MY NAME

JUDGE, JURY, & EXECUTIONER™ BOOK FIFTEEN

CRAIG MARTELLE

MICHAEL ANDERLE

CONNECT WITH THE AUTHORS

Craig Martelle Social

Website & Newsletter:
http://www.craigmartelle.com

Facebook:
https://www.facebook.com/AuthorCraigMartelle/

Michael Anderle Social

Website: http://lmbpn.com

Email List: http://lmbpn.com/email/

https://www.facebook.com/LMBPNPublishing

https://twitter.com/MichaelAnderle

https://www.instagram.com/lmbpn_publishing/

https://www.bookbub.com/authors/michael-anderle

THE SAY MY NAME TEAM

Thanks to our Beta Readers

Micky Cocker, James Caplan, Kelly O'Donnell, and John Ashmore

Thanks to the JIT Readers

Veronica Stephan-Miller
Diane L. Smith
Zacc Pelter
Daryl McDaniel
Dave Hicks
Jim Caplan
Misty Roa
Peter Manis
John Ashmore
Dorothy Lloyd
Micky Cocker
Kelly O'Donnell
Jackey Hankard-Brodie
Jeff Goode
Rachel Beckford
Larry Omans

If we've missed anyone, please let us know!

Editor
Lynne Stiegler

We can't write without those who support us
On the home front, we thank you for being there for us

We wouldn't be able to do this for a living if it weren't for our
readers
We thank you for reading our books

CHAPTER ONE

__Planet Lewbamar in the Barrier Nebula, Federation Frontier Space__

"I have brought prosperity to your city. What more do you need than that?" The voice carried a hint of danger. This wasn't a conversation with a question to be answered.

The speaker was from the bipedal Albion species, not native to Lewbamar. Malpace Frenzik led Rising Sun Industries as its chairman. The company had its fingers in all aspects of life throughout the nebula. Malpace was large even for an Albion, a humanoid race of immense proportions—two and a half meters with a chest nearly as wide.

The Lewbamarians stood half that height and had a dense coat of fur to protect them from the frigid temperatures on Lewbamar. They looked like fuzzy toys compared to the imposing Albions.

Potentate Frillbut was responsible for running the biggest city on Lewbamar. He had lost control early, resulting in a rising crime wave and increasing poverty. Over the past six months, that had turned around. Criminals worked on chain gangs, expanding the roads and nature trails in and around Crystal City.

The shine had returned to the spires. Cleaning the city was now the number one priority, which meant arrests for minor infractions and expedited trials that led to the harshest penalties. Instead of handouts, everyone seeking subsistence worked to clean the city from one end to the other. They were paid daily in food for them and their families. The hardest workers became overseers. They expected everyone to work as hard as they did.

Rising Sun Industries provided the food and the tools.

The price had been more than the city could pay.

So they'd mortgaged their future.

"It's time to pay up, Frilly," Frenzik said. He stood alone in the office with the potentate. He had dispensed with his guards since a Lewbamarian was no threat to an Albion.

The guards stood in the entry hall, where their presence alone was enough to intimidate the potentate's staff. Frenzik loved to lord his size over the smaller creatures of the nebula. He loomed over Frillbut's desk.

"It's too soon. We have a year to pay off this contract."

Frenzik huffed with impatience. He turned away and crossed his arms. He had this speech memorized from all the times he'd given it. "Allow me to draw your attention to Section One Hundred and Four, Paragraph C, Subsection Nine. What does it say?"

"There are one hundred and four sections?"

"No." Frenzik sneered. "There are two hundred and fifteen."

"We were given one hour to read and agree!"

"You could have taken all the time you felt you needed. I

had ships in the area with the necessary people and supplies, but they weren't going to stay for long. I'm sorry if you committed to something you shouldn't have. Always read the contract before you sign."

The potentate glared at the chairman. "Malpace, I only ask that you give us the one year that's detailed on the first page, and you'll get your payment. We are just now starting to realize a positive revenue. We have just signed reinvigorated trade contracts with Colay and Finx. Six more months. It's all I ask."

"Did you read *those* contracts?" Frenzik scoffed. "Frilly, please. Don't make a scene. Payment is due now. If you can't pay, then it activates Section Two Hundred. We call that the nuclear option. Your government is turned over to my people under a caretaker status until such time as the citizens of this city demonstrate they can stand on their own. All new contracts will funnel through Rising Sun Industries, which is what you agreed to when you contracted for our assistance. And of course, you'll be removed as potentate effective immediately."

"You can't do that," Frillbut howled.

"I assure you I can. The Barrier Nebula Accords enforce contract law between the member planets, and our new membership in the Federation reinforces that. We have expansive trade opportunities, Frilly. This is the renaissance of our combined planets." Frenzik waved his arms toward the ceiling. "Didn't you used to be a longshoreman? Balsik!"

The door opened, and one of the guards entered. "Mister Chairman, you called for me?"

"Frilly is no longer the potentate. Please make sure he

rejoins the workforce at the shipyard as a longshoreman. I'll fill this seat until such time as my transition team arrives." He checked the timepiece embedded in the back of his hand. "Two days. They'll be here in two days. Some people simply aren't cut out to govern themselves. Let's see what we can do to salvage the future of these poor souls."

The guard yanked Frillbut out of his chair and dragged him across the room. "You'll pay for this, Frenzik!" the Lewbamarian cried.

"Your people will say my name, not yours. I brought them peace and prosperity, not you." He waved Balsik away. "Since Crystal City has not paid me back, I'll take what they owe me—with the appropriate penalties, of course." He laughed as the former potentate was propelled through the door to land on his face. Balsik yanked him to his feet by the scruff of his neck and half-carried him out the front door.

Frenzik cracked his knuckles and took his place behind the desk. The chair was neither wide enough nor high enough for him. He grumbled as he sat with his knees jammed into the desk's underside. He pulled a personal communicator out of his pocket and set it on the desk, then brought up the hologram that represented the interface.

"Asswipe, are you there?"

"Why you gotta use such hurtful words?" the voice replied.

"How long have you known me, Ahsooleyman?" Frenzik asked.

"Infinity plus one in years, or as long as I can remember," the voice quipped. "Is it done, Malpace?"

"It is. I need you down here to set things up and make your magic happen." The chairman started to lean back, but the chair groaned and threatened to collapse. "And bring our furniture. This is Lewbamar, and these people are tiny."

"Yes, sir. I'll be on my way in minutes. I expected you would be successful, but this was fast even for you." Ahsooleyman couched his praise appropriately.

"We've never toppled a government before but let this be the first of many. Only ten member planets left in the nebula. Finding the right contracts to put into place will continue to be our greatest challenge."

"Our people are on it," Ahsooleyman replied, "with their ears to the ground."

Frenzik nodded and added, "We will find offices to help, but first, we need to control the message coming from Lewbamar. They requested our assistance, and we provided innovative and populace-friendly solutions to reduce both crime and poverty. Crystal City gleams once more! I need you to get interviews with people on the street who are as happy as bearded clams."

"I've never seen a clam," Frenzik's deputy said.

"Your loss, my friend. I must be keeping you too busy, but I don't see that changing anytime soon. Please accept my apologies now and for all time. We shan't speak of time off again."

The deputy laughed until he closed the connection. Despite Frenzik's mirth at the quick takeover, he wouldn't tolerate delay. The clock was ticking, and time was not Ahsooleyman's friend. He needed to be on the planet sooner rather than later. They both knew that.

Frenzik appreciated his deputy's attention. The right amount of joviality to celebrate success, followed by the proper dedication to getting the job done. Malpace stood and stretched. He reviewed the contract in his mind.

"For the good of all Lewbamar," he muttered. "You shall have peace and all the prosperity I will allow, more than you ever had before. We'll be long gone before you know the truth…if we ever leave."

Wyatt Earp, Azfelius, the Faerie Planet

"'Bristle Hound' has a ring to it, don't you think?" Red asked for the hundredth time. "You can call me 'BH' for short."

"I'm not calling you BH. Maybe DA, short for dumbass," Lindy shot back.

"Hey! What did I do?" He tried to look innocent, but he remained smug in that the faeries on Azfelius had allowed him on their planet after their dismissal and expulsion for being the most abrasive individual in the entire galaxy. At least he had finally grown to trust them with his son. "Why are you so angry?"

"It's been a day without Dery. I like having my son around." Der'ayd'nil, Red and Lindy's son, was conceived on Azfelius with the help of the faeries. That meant the boy was part-faerie, complete with wings and a smaller body that allowed him to fly.

"We'll get him back. They conceded that he belongs on the ship with us. They'd better, or they'll face the full wrath of the Bristle Hound, who will impart Justice on their very souls!"

Lindy rolled her eyes so hard that she lost her balance. "You won't. They'll dump your dumb ass on *Wyatt Earp's* loading ramp, just like last time."

"There were extenuating circumstances…" Red started.

"There weren't. They'll freeze your mind, then haul you off like a sack of potatoes."

Red moved in smoothly. Despite his size, he was light on his feet and extremely quick. It was his job to be agile and deadly. It was Lindy's job, too. Red wrapped up his wife in his massive arms and hugged her tightly.

"They caught me off-guard. First, I was on their planet and at their mercy. They wouldn't get away with that crap anywhere else."

"They wouldn't be anywhere else, you big goof." Lindy nuzzled his chest. "When in their house, respect their rules." She waited for a moment before adding, "BH."

Red beamed. "See how it rolls off your tongue?"

"That doesn't get Dery any closer to being with his parents. Let's try to find one of them." With the decision made, Lindy was out their door, down the passageway, and off the ship. Red hesitated, torn between getting his gear and catching up with his wife. He left the combat gear behind and ran off the ship to find Lindy outside, yelling at the sky.

"I demand to see my son!"

Red leaned against the ramp with his arms crossed and watched.

"Aren't you going to help?" Lindy snapped.

"So…" Red dragged the word out. "*I'm* the bristly one, and here you are, yelling at Mother Azfelius. The only thing you haven't done is the F-bomb. No, wait—a carpet bombing. Then your embrace of the dark side will be complete."

"What are you talking about?" Lindy waved him off, then cupped her hands around her mouth and shouted, "I said, I want to see my son!"

"How's that working for you?" Red quipped.

"Just shut up." She stomped around the green area beside the landing pad, making no sound in the soft grass. Lindy finally gave up, hung her head, and moped back to the ship.

Red didn't taunt her further. He hadn't realized how being apart from Dery was affecting her.

"What if he stays here to train as faeries are supposed to be trained? You know that we can't give him that kind of education."

Lindy turned on him, eyes on fire. She softened at his sincere look.

"But they said he needed to be with us."

"Don't make me go Neanderthal on them." Red flexed his bicep. "We'll get an answer as we get close to leaving. Speaking of, do you know when we're out of here?"

Lindy shook her head.

"What do you say we find out?" Red nodded at *Wyatt Earp* and led the way inside, took a hard right, and walked down the corridor toward the bridge, then looped down the port side of the ship where Rivka's quarters were located beyond the cargo bay.

He knocked gently on her door. After four seconds of nothing, he pounded the innocent hatch, making it shake violently.

"Butthole!" Magistrate Rivka Anoa yelled from within.

"I thought you were dead! Don't punish me for caring," Red fired back.

The door swung open to reveal Rivka in shorts and a workout shirt. "We're on Azfelius. What the hell is going to happen to me here? What do you need?"

"We want to see our son," Red admitted.

"Why the coy games? You could have simply ripped open the entire bulkhead?" Rivka smirked. She lightened up when she realized her bodyguards were serious. "We're on Azfelius. Your son is the golden child. He's what, three months old now, and already he's saved lives—our lives. They won't let anything happen to him. If there was anything to be worried about, I'd have *Wyatt Earp* in the air, and we'd be sowing devastation."

"It's not in my nature to trust the faeries," Red stated, puffing his chest out.

"Grainger is calling," Clevarious interrupted.

"I have to take this. If we get a new case, we'll collect Dery and leave."

"Mission," Red corrected.

"Case. I'm the Magistrate. I address cases and controversies. They go in a folder marked 'Cases.' If it were the 'Missions' folder, then I might think about calling them that, but it's not, so I'm not, and you shouldn't either."

"Make sure you let Erasmus know. I'm losing money in that damn pool. Can't you do what you're supposed to?"

"What the fuck are you talking about?" Rivka stood in her power stance, feet wide and fists jammed into her hips.

"Beat people up, swear at them, and arrest them! I would have made some bank on that last one if you had engaged a little more quickly."

"We didn't have a suspect!"

"But we had bets!"

"I'm not cheating so you can make money. Here's the best tip I can give you. Don't gamble. And you should be hard-blocked from the pool anyway."

"I've shed a lot of blood to feed that pool." He pulled his shirt aside to show where one of the worst scars should have been, but his nanocytes had healed him completely. His body looked as if it had never seen a bad day.

Rivka bit her lip.

"Grainger is waiting," Clevarious prompted.

"Coming!" Rivka yelled over her shoulder. "I'll tell you what I'll do. If we get through a case where zero of the lines are closed, then we get the kitty. That's a huge amount of money right now. Equal shares for everyone on the crew."

Red looked down the corridor toward the bridge.

"No," Rivka said. "Everyone is equal here, even if some spill more blood on the job than others. And what if I don't take a cut at all?"

Red rocked back. "Why would you not take a cut? Captain of the ship should get fifty percent. Everyone else gets the rest."

"You're watching too many movies. And I thought you came here to talk about your son."

Red's face fell. Rivka had distracted him. He looked at Lindy, but she gave him the stink-eye. She hadn't lost her focus.

"Let me take this call. If we need to leave, we'll contact the faeries and bring the crew back on board. I'm not sure where the Three Amigos are."

"Faerie boyfriend who looks like Adonis," Lindy said.

"Only one boyfriend for the three of them?" Rivka wondered while taking a step back to clear the doorway. "I'll never understand these modern people. How could one man handle three women?"

Red opened his mouth. Rivka looked down her nose at him. Lindy punched him in the arm, producing the dull smack of knuckles on hard flesh.

"I can't imagine," Red said. Rivka closed the door while he stood facing it. "Let's hope we get a mission. Then we'll recover our boy and be out of here."

"Do you think we're rushing him?" Lindy asked.

Red did a double-take. "Rushing Dery into what? He's three months old and already the leader of the free world."

"He is not," Lindy countered, hiding a smile behind her hand. "What am I worried about?"

Red shrugged. "Thank you for asking the last guy on this planet with the potential to answer that question."

Lindy started to laugh. "And that's why I married you. You know your limits."

"Let's get some fresh air. I can feel that we'll be leaving. It's about time, too."

CHAPTER TWO

Wyatt Earp, Azfelius, the Faerie Planet

Magistrate Grainger's mouth hung slack as if staring at a blank screen for minutes on end had taken every speck of his will to live. The scenery behind him suggested he wasn't on board his ship, but on a planet Rivka didn't recognize. His piercing blue eyes stared, unblinking.

"You've looked better," Rivka announced upon her arrival within the hologrid.

"My time is valuable, and you're on vacation. What took so long?" Grainger grumbled.

"Exactly! I'm on vacation, so sitting at the terminal waiting for your call wasn't on today's agenda. Or yesterday's, for that matter." Rivka refused to ask Grainger why he'd called. It was a game he played with her as well. He was always annoyed when she contacted him.

"The High Chancellor is thinking of retiring."

Rivka's smirk disappeared. "Good thing I'm sitting down. That's not something you drop into the middle of polite conversation."

Grainger stared out of the screen.

The higher powers moved in circles and ways Rivka had little understanding of. She didn't care, either. Her job was to deliver Justice throughout the galaxy. She had her team and loved her job. She had no designs on the position of High Chancellor.

"When do you start?" Rivka asked.

"Me? I doubt they'll want me. I'm sure senior appellate court judges are angling for the position." Grainger leaned back and looked down. "Understand that no one likes us. Our tenure as Magistrates might be coming to an end."

"That's why it needs to be you. The High Chancellor can make that happen."

"He can't. There's this convoluted approval process. Maybe the best we can hope for is that it stagnates during the process, and they don't get to it right away. I can take it as a caretaker, but that's only delaying the inevitable."

"Why is it inevitable? We've done good work keeping the Federation planets compliant and safe. Well, maybe saf*er*. There's always some jagoff who stirs up trouble, but the local authorities need something to do."

"I hope we can laugh three months from now." Grainger ran a hand through his golden-blond hair. "I don't like the machinations within the hallowed halls. It was fine when the High Chancellor was running blocker, but once he leaves, whoever is there will be at the mercy of the power class."

"From where I stand, you *are* the power class," Rivka quipped. "At least you've got time to figure it out. Stop lamenting your lease on life, grab your woman, and be an upstanding and respectable power couple."

"She's not here. On a case. My *woman*. You better not let her hear you say that." Grainger made a face.

"Clevarious, send a copy of my statement to Jael's private mail service. It's best if you send the audio. And include Grainger's directions for me not to share it."

"Of course, Magistrate. Is there anything else you'd like me to send?"

"Yes. A sympathy card, too. I feel horrible for her in this ill-fated relationship of carnal convenience. Much sympathy."

"Are you done?" Grainger asked.

"I'm just getting started!" Rivka jerked back when an orange face poked through the three-dimensional images and stepped inside the hologrid. "Wenceslaus, where'd you come from?"

"Thank the gods you've removed those cats from the High Chancellor's office. I think I'm allergic." He gave the finger to the cat.

Rivka collected her wits. "Case, Lieblen. We need a new case, or we're going to go stir-crazy. You know how vacations and I get along."

"I'm surprised you took one since they tend to cause you far more grief than relaxation. *Far* more. But since you asked, I have a little thing that just popped up…"

Wenceslaus purred while rubbing his body on Rivka's face.

"And?" she muttered around the cat.

"I sent it to you an hour ago, which tells me that you *are* enjoying your vacation. Anyway, get there as soon as you can. I'm not sure there's a crime, but it's as far from Yoll as you can get, which is a good thing. These halls of power are not being kind. We were tried by the ambassadors, and they found we do our jobs and do them well. But they remain wary. They think we're all telepaths, digging around in their minds, seeing the sordid details of their lives."

"Trust me when I tell you that's the last thing you want to see," Rivka replied.

"I'm happy not to be you. I can't imagine what you see, and I don't want to. Anyway, you have your case. Pack your shit and git."

"What language are you speaking? Did something get inside your brain and twist things around?"

"I get it. You're bored out of your mind. Bye, Rivka. Miss you already." Grainger closed the channel.

Rivka hadn't even asked where he was.

"C, what planet was he on?"

"Daedalus Prime, Magistrate," the sentient intelligence running *Wyatt Earp* replied.

"Where is that?" Rivka wondered.

"Twenty-four light-years from Yoll. It's a nearby system. There's a well-used appellate court there for off-world issues."

"Appellate courts. They get to second-guess every facet of the prosecution's existence. I'm glad I don't have to deal with them."

"Don't they ensure the law is applied equally?"

"Supposedly," Rivka grudgingly admitted. "Still glad I don't have to deal with them. And once a capital crime is adjudicated, it isn't reversible. That's why I touch them, no matter how horrific it is to be in their minds. I have to be sure, and it has to be final. I can't watch a perp walk free. Not ever again."

Rivka's mood had soured, so the big orange cat scratched her as he jumped down. She opened the file Grainger had sent. Lewbamar. Crystal City had been taken over by a foreign corporation for failure to pay their debt. The former potentate had filed the complaint with the Federation.

"Why in the hell is this on my desk? When you don't pay your bills, you get to pay the piper instead. My initial impression is that this guy signed a bad contract. What does Grainger know that I don't?"

"I don't know what Grainger knows, or you, for that matter, so I cannot compare the two knowledge bases to answer your question. Please accept my most sincere apologies," Clevarious told her.

Rivka closed the hologrid to find Wenceslaus sitting on her pillow on the couch, licking his butt.

Doctor Tyler Toofakre propped an elbow on their bed and watched her. "Tell me we're getting out of here."

"Call the team to the conference room. I want to talk with everyone about this upcoming case, and then we're getting out of here." She winked at the guy the crew called "Man Candy." He took it well, giving as good as he got with scalpel-like accuracy. He had also saved most of their lives during his time with them. He was the ship's doctor.

Maybe they should have called him "Bones." They still could. Rivka looked at him for a moment, then winked. "You better get dressed. People will talk."

She looked at her clothes and decided to change as well.

She dropped what she was wearing in the middle of the floor. From her small wardrobe, she selected one of her suits, a garment she wore when she was lawyering. She caressed the leather of her Magistrate's jacket before deciding to leave it in the closet. She'd break it out when conditions outside the ship weren't as tropical as they were on Azfelius.

"What's the weather like in Crystal City on Lewbamar?" Rivka asked.

"Cold. A warm day is ten degrees Celsius. It is usually around freezing or colder," Clevarious replied. Rivka smiled and closed the wardrobe to find Tyler standing there naked. "What the hell?"

"Catching a quick shower. Two minutes. It's all I take. I'm not like…" He thought better of finishing the sentence. Rivka loved long, hot showers. "Clevarious is recalling the team. Sahved is nearby. Red, Lindy, and the SCAMPs are on board. The others are outside. I have time."

"Sounds like everyone I need is on board except for Sahved. I could have used a shower before I got dressed. I probably should have taken one while Grainger was waiting."

Tyler pointed with his head toward the bathroom.

"Two minutes? I deserve better than that, even if *you're* good with it. It's not a race."

"I concur. Thirty minutes, no less. Tonight, under the starlit sky of a frigid Lewbamar, I shall court you appropriately."

"It's a date." Rivka headed toward the door. "Get cleaned up while I chase people down. I swear, sometimes they're like toddlers."

Rivka stepped into the corridor and almost ran into

Clodagh walking by, carrying Alanna. "I heard there's a meeting. Do you need me?"

"Negatory. We'll be talking about the legal elements of this upcoming case. I'm not convinced there's been a crime. Grainger is sure there has. We have to check it out. Set course for Lewbamar in the Barrier Nebula."

Clodagh scrunched her face as she tried to remember her star charts. "That's way the hell across the galaxy. Are they Federation?"

"Recent addition. Let's show the flag and make them feel good about their decision to join, or I might have to start offing people."

Clodagh frowned. "Really?"

"No." Rivka clapped Clodagh on the shoulder. "Where's Tiny Man Titan or Floyd?"

"Probably with Wenceslaus." She waved in all directions. "Out there."

"The big orange is in my quarters, being a nuisance," Rivka replied. They walked toward the bridge, Clodagh putting a spring in her step to bounce the baby. "Aren't you afraid Titan will run away?"

"He runs and runs, he's so happy, and the faeries always bring him back." Clodagh cooed to Alanna.

"Summon the tiny dog wranglers because we're going to get going fairly soon. And if you talk to the faeries, make sure they know to bring Dery back. His parents might go scorched earth on Azfelius if we try to leave without him."

"I'll contact Flight Control and see what I can do. Scorched earth. I believe they would. Same thing I'd do if they tried to keep Alanna, but they've been nothing but kind to her and us."

"Enjoy your time with Cole. I don't see any reason for him to join us." Rivka looked at the overhead and yelled, "Conference room for the legal team!"

Have you forgotten about your internal comm chip? Clevarious asked in Rivka's mind.

"Of course not, but this is my ship, and Terry Henry Walton called yelling his 'Marine Corps intercom,' wherever that came from. It's good for the lungs."

"I think a cardio workout is good for the lungs," Clevarious replied.

"Pshaw, C. Let me find Sahved." Rivka hurried around the corner and toward the airlock.

"I've already called him. He's on his way."

"What if I want to go outside?" Rivka asked. "There is nowhere nicer than Azfelius."

Clevarious played classical music over the ship's sound system. Pachelbel's *Canon*. "Then why weren't you outside to begin with?" Clevarious asked while the D Major version filled the ship.

"Because I don't want to be spoiled. I might find a place I never want to leave, and what good would that do the universe? Justice is calling my name."

Ankh'Po'Turn, Crenellian and ambassador at large, stepped through the hatch from the engineering spaces he claimed as his workshop. "We need materials from Lewbamar," he told Rivka in an even tone while staring at the Magistrate. After thirty seconds of not blinking, he returned to his workshop.

She hadn't bothered asking for an explanation.

"There is no such place," Clevarious continued.

"What are you talking about? Lewbamar just joined the

Federation, and we owe them a duty of due care." She waved dismissively and headed outside.

I mean, a place you may never want to leave. You already have that, and it's called Wyatt Earp. *You can lie to me and the others, but you can't lie to yourself.*

Rivka leaned against the bulkhead within the airlock. She was always surrounded by people, but people of her choosing. She rarely had time to herself to contemplate something as complex as what she wanted to do with the rest of her life.

Even now, Clevarious would be listening.

"I don't know what else I want out of life. It's not the High Chancellor's position. I'm happy for Grainger. He'll be fine once he figures it out."

"The High Chancellor is leaving?" Sahved asked from the ramp leading into the ship. "That is disconcerting. He had clout, the most clout of anyone ever and then some."

Rivka chuckled. "Your inner Yemilorian is getting out."

"It so very much escapes. I must apologize like has never before been apologized for such extreme indiscretions!" Sahved winked. "Ever."

"That's more like it. All is forgotten. Conference room. I'll be along in a minute. Have C pull up the package on Lewbamar. This is a hide-and-seek. Try to find the crime, Sahved."

"No crime will go unsolved, Magistrate!" he declared, pumping his fist, only to hit the overhead within the airlock chamber. "Ouch."

He rubbed his three-fingered hand.

"We shall figure it out," he said and continued inside the ship.

Rivka chuckled to herself while shaking her head. This was her team. Sahved was a skilled investigator. He saw things the others did not, so she was happy to have him. He could also climb like a chimpanzee, which had helped the team when they were stranded on the planet called Tanglewood.

She walked slowly down the ramp, breathing deeply of the fresh overgrowth. Sandalwood and Ikenberry. She closed her eyes to concentrate on the scent. When she opened them again, she couldn't remember how much time had passed. Azfelius didn't do time like normal planets.

A vine crept along one of *Wyatt Earp's* landing struts.

"Guys?" she called. "We're gearing up to head out. Got a planet to save." She didn't add "from itself."

She was convinced this was a ploy to get her out of the Federation limelight during the time of change. The High Chancellor was retiring? She still couldn't wrap her head around it. Lewbamar signed a bad contract. They'd know better next time. Who would she have to berate about it before moving on?

Whee! a little girl's voice cried into her mind.

Rivka braced herself as the wombat burst through the foliage and zigzagged toward the ramp. It was wide but never wide enough when Floyd was on a tear. The wombat accelerated, her thick back legs driving her round body forward. She headed straight for Rivka, who was dancing back and forth, trying to gauge where Floyd would hit.

She miscalculated because the big girl jumped rather than ran low. Rivka stumbled backward and was off-balance when the heavy creature hit her mid-chest. The

Magistrate went down hard and slammed into the ramp, the wind leaving her chest in an explosive grunt.

Love! Floyd cried while sniffing Rivka's face with her snout dangerously close to her mouth. Rivka bench-pressed the wombat into the air and rolled sideways to deposit her on the ramp.

"I love you, too, Floyd. Did you have a good time?"

Go?

"Yes, little girl. It's time for us to get going. If you're hungry, run into the brush and graze one last time. The food onboard the ship is nowhere near as good."

Floyd hesitated for a moment, then raced down the ramp and across the small grassy field and disappeared into the heavy brush.

Rivka took one more deep breath. Even with the nanocytes and her fitness, her chest hurt from the impact with the flying wombat.

Floyd didn't fly, but she could jump higher than Rivka had realized.

Must be the clean living.

Rivka didn't even get to the grass before returning to the ship to find Red and Lindy waiting. The Magistrate didn't wait for them to ask. "No sign of the faeries. Clodagh called them for us." She gestured for them to follow. "Briefing room."

They trooped the corridors of *Wyatt Earp*, heading for the conference room. Sentient intelligences Chaz and Dennicron, in their self-contained artificial mobility plat-forms, would join them. Sahved was already there, sitting awkwardly at the table.

Tyler was by one of the seats. "If Lauton and Groenwyn show up, I'll stand."

Chaz and Dennicron appeared in the doorway. Chaz raised one finger to draw the group's attention. "We are sorry for our tardiness. We were having sex."

Rivka recoiled and made her best horrified face. "No one needs to know that."

"It was invigorating, yet oddly relaxing," Dennicron explained.

"Stop," Rivka pleaded.

"Most gratifying!" Chaz and Dennicron looked at each other and nodded.

"Stop. Please, before I puke," Rivka begged.

"Humans!" the SIs said in unison, followed by another synchronized head nod.

Rivka shook off the attempt of her SIs to shock their flesh and blood counterparts. "We could use Lauton and Groenwyn," Rivka continued. "Maybe that's the crime—white-collar finance if this company cheated the city government to activate some contract clause. I don't know. I'm grasping at straws. We're starting without much information, and I don't see any of it as a crime."

"Speaking of having no information," Sahved started, "it's like I joined in the middle of the briefing. What city government? Where are we going?"

"I'm sorry. Let me start at the beginning. On Lewbamar in the Barrier Nebula. Crystal City is the main urban area, and it seems that the city government has had the city repossessed by a lender. Now they're pissed off."

"I am sorry, but what are the charges?" Chaz asked.

"This is the first time we've gone somewhere when

there isn't clear evidence of a crime. Hell, there isn't even the implication of a crime except in the mind of a city government official who lost his job," Rivka replied. "We'll go in on a fact-finding mission. C, what should we expect from the locals?"

"They are very much like our precious Floyd, fuzzy and round, but they walk upright. They speak a common language. Your chips will interpret instantly as usual. The corporation that has taken over is called Rising Sun Industries. Its chairman is Malpace Frenzik. He's from Albion, a race of giants, humanoids approximately two and a half meters tall but wide chests, double those of a comparably sized human."

"Giants versus the fuzzballs." Rivka rubbed her temples.

"Groenwyn will be most pleased with the Lewbamarians. She has a soft spot for the fur-coated," Sahved suggested.

Rivka stopped rubbing her temples long enough to stare at Sahved, who had already lost focus. It was hard to keep them on track when Rivka wasn't convinced they would have work to do beyond asking a few questions.

"Clodagh, any word from the faeries?" Rivka asked while looking at the holographic projection of Lewbamar spinning over the middle of the table.

"They are on their way with all parties, including Dery."

Red hugged Lindy to him. He wasn't ready for her to make war on the faeries.

Turnabout. It was an enlightened day when Red was the voice of reason.

"I'll meet our hosts for an official goodbye. Sahved, review the case notes with Chaz and Dennicron. There might be a minor crime, but is it enough to void a contract with an offer and acceptance with an exchange of consideration? We'll get a copy of the full contract from the Lewbamarians for further detailed examination." Rivka twirled her finger in the air. "Saddle up, people. Next stop is Lewbamar."

She worked her way out of the small conference room and hurried to the airlock. Red and Lindy followed her.

"All's well that ends well," Rivka said over her shoulder.

"I like my son," Lindy said, not as an excuse but as a statement of fact. "Which means I like having him around. He's three months old and not quite ready to go off on his own, no matter what he looks like."

The last time Rivka had seen him, he'd looked to be a ten-year-old. After a few days with the faeries, she didn't know what to expect.

She nodded, not voicing her concern. Speculating added no value. They'd deal with whatever the faeries would drop on them. Rivka had to trust that the faeries had her and her team's best interests at heart. For that matter, they seemed to want the best for the galaxy as long as no one interfered with them.

Dery would be their ambassador. Rivka was sure of it.

Lindy only wanted her little boy back.

They waited on the grass outside for the faeries to appear. First to arrive was the hulking male who easily carried the three pilots. He placed them gently on the grass and blew kisses as he retreated into the air. The three delivered swoon-worthy testimonials of their undying love. After he was out of sight, they collected themselves and headed for the ship.

"Magistrate," Aurora said matter-of-factly on her way past.

"Men in the rest of the universe don't have a chance?" Rivka quipped.

"Oh, no. We'll hold them to a higher standard, that's all." The three hurried into the ship, giggling the whole way.

Next to arrive were Groenwyn and Lauton. "Good! We need your forensic accounting experience," Rivka called as the two faeries carrying them deposited them on the grass. The women bowed deeply. The faeries dipped their heads in response and flew away.

"Sounds good," Lauton said. She took Groenwyn's hand, and they strolled up the ramp.

"We're going to Lewbamar, where the inhabitants are short, round, and covered in fur, or so I'm told."

Groenwyn smiled. "I look forward to meeting them. How could such creatures commit crimes?" Her expression changed to one of concern.

"The crime is alleged to have been committed by a race of humanoid giants against the Lewbamarians, and we need to find out what happened. Sahved, Chaz, and Denni-cron will bring you up to speed. And if you want your day ruined, ask them about their latest dalliance, which they described as both invigorating and calming."

Groenwyn took Rivka by the shoulders. "Some things don't need to be shared, Magistrate."

"Tell *them* that!"

"But since you did, good for them!" Groenwyn stepped back and shouted, "Where's my little girl?"

Rivka pointed at the brush. Groenwyn turned around and saw the wombat burst through the foliage and race toward the ramp. Rivka hoisted herself onto the rail to avoid the incoming wombat missile. Groenwyn took a knee and welcomed her friend with a deft twist to catch her sideways instead of receiving Floyd's full momentum.

Lauton kneeled beside the pair and scratched behind Floyd's stubby ears. A minute later, the three happily trotted into the ship.

The last group to arrive represented a full delegation led by Siro'ti'lc. She settled to the ground first.

Rivka didn't have to look to know that her bodyguards were upset.

"Where's Dery?"

Der'ayd'nil is coming. He is completing the final phase of his training, Siro'ti'lc replied.

"He's done with his training?" Rivka held up her hand to keep Lindy and Red behind her.

Oh, no. The faerie laughed. *Just this part. Please bring him home to us as often as you can. There is so much more for him to learn.*

"His home is on *Wyatt Earp*," Red growled.

Of course, it is. We are a second home to him. I hope we don't alienate you to where you don't want to return. That wouldn't be good for the boy.

Lindy forced her way past Rivka. She bowed to the faerie before speaking in measured tones. "What about us? What steps are you taking not to alienate us?" Lindy asked.

Siro'ti'lc fluttered her wings to move forward. She reached out a delicate hand to take Lindy's. The two communed without words for a few moments. *Do you understand?*

"I do and thank you. I hope that you understand us, too.

We need to know and would like to be there for his future training, to include taking the training ourselves."

Siro'ti'lc glanced at Red, who was flexing his muscles in response to the tension he felt.

Not him, the faerie said. She didn't bother saying who. There was no doubt that she was referring to the bristle hound.

The other faeries settled into the glen, arrayed around the group of humans but not too close. Rivka crossed her arms and tapped her foot on the metal of the ramp.

Siro'ti'lc pointed skyward. In the distance, three faeries flew toward them.

No, only two. Between them flew a child, the one Rivka remembered. Lindy bounced in anticipation.

Red thumped down the ramp to join his wife. He stared into the sky while Rivka watched the faeries. They were focused on the parents.

Lindy and Red.

CHAPTER THREE

The two escorts peeled off to allow Dery to fly himself the last hundred meters. He glided downward and over the heads of the delegation led by the meditator, Siro'ti'lc.

He backwinged at the last moment to stop in mid-air. Lindy caught him and pulled him to her. She held him tightly while kissing his head.

Mother! the boy said happily into their minds. *Father!*

Red moved close. Their previous angst was gone.

The faeries watched intently.

"We'll be on our way," Rivka interrupted.

Siro'ti'lc moved close to Rivka and said in her soft thought voice, *Take care with him. He processes trauma differently than you and his parents. They thrive on conflict. He loses a part of himself with each hostile act he is exposed to. Please, shield him from that.*

Our ability to deal with conflict makes us stronger. Dery has already shown that he understands what we do and, most importantly, why we do it. He will remain integral if that's what his parents decide. Wouldn't it be great if we could all avoid conflict? But that's not what's going on out there.

Rivka pointed toward space. *We can't hide on a shielded planet. The battle is out there, and we must win if we're to leave the galaxy a better place than we found it. That's what Dery can do. Maybe his calling is higher than you imagine.*

Siro'ti'lc lifted into the air. *Keep him safe, Rivka Anoa. For all our sakes.*

Rivka replied out loud, "We will do everything we can to keep him safe while still doing our jobs of making the Federation a safer place. We all seem to have a higher calling, Meditator. How we answer shows our commitment to a greater good."

The faeries filled the sky. Dery pulled free from his mother's grip so he could join his fellows for one last whirl. They flew in a tight circle before the faeries gained altitude and angled toward the horizon. Dery circled downward.

"Come on, son. Let's go home," Red said in his fatherly voice. It sounded different from his usual gruff tone. He waved for the boy to follow. Lindy let Dery follow his father while she kept the child from flying out from between them. The boy dive-bombed his dad's head and wrapped his legs around Red's neck, then tucked his wings against his back and enjoyed the ride.

Rivka waited until they were inside before taking one last look at Azfelius.

He is greater than you know. Greater than any of us, but only if he reaches his full potential, the faerie meditator said.

"I believe that of all our children," Rivka replied. "Titan! You little bastard, get in the ship right now!"

Despite claims to the contrary, the faeries had not brought him back.

He's with Clodagh on the bridge, Clevarious said.

"Why the hell are we still here, then? Let's get this parade on the road!" Rivka jogged up the ramp and into the ship. Before she punched the button to close the outer hatch, the ramp was already retracting. She hammered the big red button and headed for her quarters.

It was time to don her Magistrate's jacket and let the legal power flow through her.

It made her feel the authority of her office.

Planet Lewbamar in the Barrier Nebula, Federation Frontier Space

"Welcome to Crystal City!" a pleasant voice greeted. "Please descend along the indicated route and land next to the city office complex. We look forward to your visit."

The channel closed. Kennedy transferred the controls to manual and took *Wyatt Earp* into the upper atmosphere.

"Doesn't sound like a city in distress," Rivka muttered. "Let's see… Lauton, Groenwyn, Chaz, Dennicron, Sahved, and Red, meet me at the airlock, ready to go. Red, full gear."

"Hang on!" Lindy yelled from down the corridor. A flutter of wings preceded her arrival on the bridge. She blocked the hatch with her arms crossed while Dery made a circuit of the interior, finally opting to land on the armrest of the captain's chair. Tiny Man Titan wagged his tail furiously while trying to climb Clodagh's chest to get closer to Dery.

"You just got your son back. I thought you'd want to spend some time with him."

"He's back, and he'll be waiting when we return. I still need to do my job."

Rivka thought about saying that her job would be what the Magistrate said it was, but that wouldn't be helpful. "Full gear, then. Five minutes before we land."

Lindy blew a kiss at her son and hurried away.

"Are you okay staying here with your aunties?" Rivka asked.

"He is a pleasure to be around. He calms everything down. Don't you?"

Dery replied, *Peace is nourishment for the soul.*

Rivka knew she should have been surprised at the boy spouting philosophy at three months of age, but she wasn't. Very little surprised her when it came to her crew.

"What about me?" Tyler asked from the corridor.

"I don't see any blood, running, swearing, or arrests on this case. Set up a free dental clinic out of the cargo hold if you want. Clodagh and her people will help you get the word out."

"It's been a while. I'll look up Lewbamarian dental conditions right away. Thanks, babe." He ran off.

Rivka looked at her jacket to reaffirm her station. There was the pin, the scales of Justice.

"I used to be somebody." She sighed. "Now Grainger has me chasing ghosts."

"You are well-respected throughout the galaxy," Clevarious murmured into the silence. "I meant the whole universe."

"C, you've no need to butter my muffin, but I appreciate it."

"Butter your muffin?" the SI repeated. "I don't know where to start to parse that. Does anyone know?"

Aurora shook her head. Clodagh shrugged. Dery picked up Titan and flew him around the bridge before returning him to the chief engineer's lap.

Rivka held up her hands. "Hopefully, we won't be long." She stepped into the corridor and shouted, "Everyone who's going ashore, meet me at the airlock in fifteen seconds!"

Clevarious relayed the call to make sure everyone heard. "They are on their way, Magistrate."

Red jingled as he walked toward her. "Why are you making so much noise?"

"Intimidation factor. Heavy metal is coming to ruin your day."

"I'm not intimidated since I know I can take you."

"If it makes you feel better to think that, then fine." Red backtracked to the airlock. "But it's not you I'm leaning on. It's the three-meter-tall Albions. They probably aren't used to seeing a total specimen like me."

Rivka blinked as she tried to understand the jumble of words that had cascaded from Red's mouth. She should have known better.

The ship continued its descent to the planet's surface. The air lanes were clear to a small landing pad within a double-fenced compound. *Wyatt Earp* angled to make room for the tethered runabout, *Destiny's Vengeance*. Ankh's ship traveled with the heavy frigate but outside since there was no room for a ship that big in the cargo bay.

The ships settled to the ground. *Wyatt Earp* powered down and extended the ramp. Rivka signaled, and Red elbowed the big red button to open the hatch. A frigid gust blew through the opening.

Groenwyn groaned. They had just departed a tropical paradise with always-perfect temperatures. Experiencing the cold less than an hour later was a shock.

The hatch to Engineering opened, and Ankh strolled out to take his place with the group.

"What are you doing?"

"I'm coming along. Erasmus wants us to be more involved, especially with new planets. The Singularity has no presence on any planet in the Barrier Nebula."

"Fine." Rivka was happy that the ambassadors were joining them. They would be able to talk with any system the Lewbamarians maintained. When it came to digging into the deepest, darkest hiding places, there was no one better than Ankh.

"We are ecstatic that you are joining us," Dennicron added. Ankh stared at her without blinking but didn't reply.

"Time to go, people," Rivka prodded.

Red left first, stopping just outside the hatch and slowly taking in the area. The welcome committee stood on a sidewalk beyond the end of the ramp. The sidewalk stretched to the right, where the largest of the compound's buildings stood. The area was protected by a substantial security fence. He couldn't see any weapons or places for a sniper to hide.

He continued down the ramp, gratified by the looks of concern on the delegation's faces. Half a dozen locals waved, the fur on their small arms flowing with their gestures. Two giants stood behind them. Albions. They looked like Greek gods with tanned skin and tight clothes that stretched with each movement, accentuating the musculature beneath.

Sahved went next, then Groenwyn and Lauton. Rivka fell in behind them. Ankh joined her. Chaz and Dennicron brought up the rear, with Lindy appearing to meander away from the group.

The largest of the two Albions called, "My name is Ahsooleyman. Welcome to beautiful Lewbamar." His voice projected without shouting.

The locals wore genuine smiles.

"I'm not feeling the crime," Rivka whispered to Sahved.

"I shall reserve judgment," the Yemilorian replied.

"They seem happy to me," Groenwyn added. "If all the people we dealt with were this happy, the galaxy would be a pretty good place."

Rivka moved to the front until she was even with Red. *I'm going to shake all their hands, but especially the Albions.*

"Roger," Red replied softly out of the side of his mouth.

The delegation eased forward as Rivka got close.

"My name is Buffloll, but call me Buffy," a Lewbamarian said, stepping forward and offering a furry hand. Rivka took it and the local giggled. "I am the head of the Human Resources Department."

In her mind, Rivka saw peace and warmth, the end of strife. She was content. "Thank you, Buffy. I'm Magistrate Rivka Anoa." She continued down the line and received similar images from the rest of the locals. Rivka found it refreshing. Too often, she was thrust into the middle of a fraught situation.

When she reached the Albion who called himself Ahsooleyman, she took a moment to size him up. "You're a big one," she remarked before holding out her hand.

The Albion held his hands up. "We do not shake hands. Our strength has a tendency to break things that are best not broken."

"I think you'll find that we're hardier creatures than what you're used to." Rivka kept her hand extended.

"As you wish." The Albion took her hand but didn't squeeze hard. Rivka held tightly, but her hand barely extended beyond his palm. In his alien mind floated wisps of truth. The lesser races needed to be handled gently. Delivering security and adding prosperity. Malpace was doing them a favor.

"How did Lewbamar come to have such a crime problem?" Rivka asked. The Lewbamarians sighed and looked at the ground.

The Albion responded, "That is difficult to answer since we've only been here for six months, but gangs, drugs, and bad influences twisted the youth away from the path of peace and prosperity. Parents lost control. We helped train law enforcement to crack down. We established a holistic approach to life where jobs were integral to purpose. Once the youth found they mattered, the ill-fated attention-seeking, and if I may add, self-destructive behaviors, quickly disappeared."

"Sounds like work will set you free, a slogan that delivered exactly the opposite on Earth."

"The proof is in the results. The people are free to walk

the streets. Alas, there is still some crime, but we are quickly wiping that out. Next step is an intergalactic conglomerate headquartered right here. Lewbamarian crystals on every hand, in every heart, and the foundation of discerning portfolios Federation-wide!" He delivered the last of his sales pitch with a flourish.

"Are you a salesman or a city administrator?" Rivka asked with a half-smile.

"In Rising Sun Industries, we've found that an integrated and balanced work and home life is optimal for society. A work balance means a product that we don't sell to each other but to those throughout the galaxy. Everyone here already has family crystals, but we think there is a broader and more vibrant market out there."

Rivka swallowed hard, refusing to look at Red, who was trying to get her attention.

"What I hear you saying," Red started. Rivka closed her eyes and bit the inside of her cheek. She knew what was coming. "Is that you're going to show your family jewels throughout the Federation."

"We have the best family jewels. Yes! Better than crystals. Family jewels, straight from the caves of Lewbamar."

Rivka stabbed a finger at Red to keep him from digging deeper.

"I recommend not using 'family jewels.' It's already trademarked and cliché." Rivka waved dismissively.

"I have to ask, Magistrate. Why are you here? We never received any notice about your trip or the purpose of it," Ahsooleyman said.

"The transfer of authority from an elected government to a private entity due to a contract breach is unprecedented. They sent me to look into it, that's all. I'm as much at a loss as you are. I look forward to learning more about your wonderful city." Rivka stepped back to gaze over the razor-wire-topped barrier between the compound and the metropolis.

"We would love to have a banquet tonight in your honor." Ahsooleyman bowed. Even bent in half, he towered over the heads of the Lewbamarians. Red looked up at the Albion, who smiled in return.

Rivka nodded at the other non-Lewbamarian.

"I'm Belloward, assistant to Mr. Ahsooleyman. I'll take care of any requests you have. In the interim, I suggest we allow this august group of leaders to get back to work. If you'll come with me, I'll show you to the archives, where you may review any records you wish."

"We'll need a copy of that contract," Rivka said as an oh-by-the-way in her effort not to add friction. "Where are my manners? Let me introduce my team. Ambassador at Large Ankh'Po'Turn from Crenellia, and inside his head, he carries Ambassador Erasmus, leader of the Singularity. This tall fellow is Sahved, a Yemilorian."

"Shorty," the Albion greeted Sahved.

"We have no family jewels," Sahved stated. Red quickly turned away, cheek muscles flexing as he clenched his jaw tightly.

"Groenwyn and Lauton," Rivka continued. "Chaz and Dennicron."

She didn't describe anyone's function on the team because she didn't want to show her hand. Not yet. She didn't know why, but she felt something wasn't right.

What if the people were under undue influence? They

looked and seemed far too happy. That would render a contract signed under such conditions null and void.

And the finances. How did a private corporation fund a law enforcement intervention and jobs for misguided youth? How did that work? Had there been that much mismanagement before they came?

"Dammit," she mumbled. "We're going to be here for a while."

Magistrate? Sahved asked, but she shook her head. He waited. She needed to concentrate. They'd be able to talk privately soon, and she could pace as she knew she'd need to.

CHAPTER FOUR

Crystal City Archives, Planet Lewbamar in the Barrier Nebula

The archives looked like a contemporary Federation library but were bustling with activity. There were very few old-fashioned books since trees, and sources for pulp to make paper were sparse. Anything grown was used to feed the population. The research positions consisted of computerized viewers with oversized screens to replicate reading a print copy of the material. When there hadn't been so many Lewbamarians, there had been a robust printing industry heavily supported by recycling, so old books had become new pulp and new books. Now, it was rare to have anything in a physical form.

Rivka sat at the offered terminal, and Belloward brought up the contract.

"Please transmit this to my office as well. I'll need to have a copy in my files."

"Everything you need is right here," the Albion countered.

"Everything except a case file to present to the Federation's High Chancellor. If I'm to dismiss this case, then I need to present evidence. That means I need original or certified documents that I can accept into evidence. This is what's called the discovery phase. We collect information about the issue."

"What was the issue again?" Belloward stood his ground.

"Contract law. Duly elected governments do not get replaced by corporations. That's our starting point. The good news is that Rising Sun Industries does not have to prove its innocence. It's my job to prove their guilt. Now, you'll need to transmit that file and leave us alone. Otherwise, I'll have to detain you for interfering in my investigation."

"Please, no!" The Albion stumbled backward. "That isn't my intent at all."

Rivka popped up from her seat and hurried after him. She grabbed his hand, ostensibly to keep him from falling. *Help but don't go out of your way. Try to give them nothing...* His instructions had been clear.

The Magistrate let go of his hand and waved him away. "We'll call if we need something. I expect to see that file arrive within the next five minutes so my team still on board my ship can review it separately."

"I'll get right on it." He bowed deeply, which brought his head even with Rivka's. She stared him down since he didn't break eye contact. After he hurried away, she resumed her seat.

The team crowded around her while Red and Lindy made sure there was plenty of room between the Magistrate and the working Lewbemarians. They got the hint and moved to the far side of the room.

Ankh pulled out his toolkit and conducted a quick scan of the space. He put one of his interface discs on the side of the computer terminal. Three seconds later, his eyes refocused. "We have all the files, and there are no intrusion devices. The video cameras watching this area have been disabled."

With their privacy assured, Rivka spoke. "Thank you for coming, Ankh and Erasmus. You've already been a great help." She turned to address the rest of the team. "I didn't see anything in Asshole Man's mind that looked like guilt or admission of a crime. In Blowhard's, he was instructed to give us the minimal help possible. If they are so open, why would they tell him that?"

Chaz raised a hand. "Not allowing a fishing expedition is fully compliant with Federation law. We need probable cause to look at anything outside the contract unless there is something in the contract that we can use for search warrants into other aspects of this business arrangement. Dennicron and I have already reviewed this contract..."

"Of course you have. I might need a little more time." Rivka glanced at the screen. "Two hundred and forty pages. What a nightmare."

"It is heavily one-sided," Chaz stated.

"No shit." Rivka wasn't surprised. "But is there anything in there that is patently illegal under Federation law? Bad and lopsided contracts are not illegal. Was there consideration? Was there an offer and an acceptance? Were there consequences for both parties for failure to perform?"

"All of that, although the consequences for Rising Sun

are limited to Crystal City paying actual costs should there have been early termination or failure to meet crime reduction targets."

"Rising Sun met the targets?" Rivka asked.

"They reached the targets eight months early and exceeded them by an additional fifty percent at six months, which triggered the requirement for a windfall payout despite the contract being predicated on twelve months. Failure to make payment carried the harshest penalty: turn over city management and all finances to Rising Sun Industries."

Rivka shook her head. Chaz mirrored her movements until she pointed at him. "Stop that." She sucked on her teeth while contemplating her next moves. "Chaz and Dennicron, research Lewbamarian law regarding the city officials' standing to make such a contract. Was the city theirs to barter with, especially the finances? There are usually controls saying exactly who can spend the citizens' money. I've never seen a case where it wasn't a governmental body."

The SCAMPs nodded. "Your wish is our command."

"Why do you two keep tinkering with your protocols?"

"It's the sex, isn't it?" Dennicron replied. Rivka dug her thumbs into her temples and slowly rotated them to relieve the pressure building within her brain.

"That's exactly it." Rivka surrendered. "Back to the ship and get on the deep research. Lindy, you stay here with Lauton. Pull the financial data for a solid timeframe leading up to the contract with Rising Sun. Whatever you recommend. Three years, five years. Makes no difference to me.

Baseline the numbers and then look into the timeframe following implementation of the contract with Rising Sun. I suspect Crystal City had no way of paying the bill.

"Sahved, I need you to find Potentate Frillbut and discuss all of this with him. If he signed a bad contract simply out of expediency, he'll lie about it."

"I would expect," Sahved agreed.

"Take Groenwyn with you, and make sure she doesn't get hurt. Take Lindy, too. Lauton, return to the ship with Chaz and Dennicron and do your work from there. I believe we have all the files." Rivka looked at Ankh.

"All of them," Ankh confirmed.

"Red, Ankh, and I will discuss the meaning of life with our Albion hosts." Rivka powered down the terminal and stood. She stretched as if she'd spent longer than thirty seconds sitting. "You have your marching orders. I think we'll be able to declare that contract null and void, limiting it to payment for services rendered and canceling out the complete surrender of the city. Sahved, we'll get Barrow Head to take you."

"Belloward," Sahved corrected.

"That's what I said," Rivka replied.

"But it's not…"

Red nudged him. "Give it up, Shorty. You won't win those arguments with the Magistrate."

"There's no argument. She's mispronouncing their names. Accuracy is important. And how did my name become 'Shorty?'"

"In documentation, accuracy is critical." Rivka gave Sahved two thumbs-up.

"See?" Red elbowed him again before leading the team to the exit, jingling all the way.

Rivka made eye contact with Lindy, who returned her best helpless look. "You married him."

"You hired him."

"I guess we're both stuck." Lindy scanned the archives. All eyes were on the group of foreigners. Lindy didn't think any of those watching looked threatening. She kept her eyes moving, checking for weapons, but the Lewbamarians appeared to be nothing more than stuffed animals. It seemed odd that there had been a crime wave. They radiated happiness, not unlike Floyd.

Red powered through the door and ran chest-first into Belloward. He stopped instantly, but the Albion didn't budge. "You're leaving already?" the assistant asked.

"We are breaking into teams to expedite the discovery process." Rivka pointed at the groups. "That bunch is going back to the ship. This group here is going into town, and I'll need you to take them. They have to interview the former potentate. Frillbut, I believe. And the final three need to talk with Mr. Ahsooleyman, and then we'll need to talk with Mr. Frenzik."

"Chairman Frenzik has returned to Albion. He is unavailable, but we can facilitate a phone call with him."

Rivka rubbed her chin while nodding thoughtfully. She removed her datapad and contacted Clevarious. "C, prepare a subpoena to compel Malpace Frenzik to return to Lewbamar immediately to provide testimony in this case. And add a second subpoena for all communications related to the contract with Crystal City."

"You can't make him do that," Belloward stated matter-of-factly.

Rivka held his gaze. "I assure you that I can. Failure to comply with a judge-issued subpoena risks losing your assets. As chairman of Rising Sun Industries, I think his assets are rather substantial. That is a huge bet to place on guaranteed failure."

"I don't understand."

"Federation law. You should familiarize yourself with it since Albion is a member of the Federation, as is Lewbamar. Whatever Wild West you were running out here before the Barrier Nebula planets joined no longer applies. Why did Albion join the Federation?"

"Defense pact. We're at the edge of known space, which means everything beyond is more than happy to stop by and take potshots. We might be strong in person, but our space fleet is not. We fear for our planet."

"Then you won't want to risk it by Mr. Frenzik ignoring a subpoena."

"I'll have to transmit messages. Please wait." Belloward hurried away, leaving the group outside. The wind had a bite to it, but even Ankh had gone into the Pod-doc to get nanocytes to strengthen his body. They weren't immune but also weren't bothered by minor discomforts like a chill.

"Return to the ship. You have work you can do." Rivka waved the SCAMPs and Lauton away.

Lauton gave Groenwyn a quick peck on the cheek before hurrying after Chaz and Dennicron.

The team looked at each other while Red and Lindy faced away from them. Ankh stared without blinking.

"You're going to ask them to add an SI to their planet's information systems, aren't you?"

Ankh didn't answer, but Erasmus did, *While we're here. I have people who are out of work. They need places to set up shop. Earn their livelihoods.*

Despite Rivka's defense and approval, she had a hard time getting her head around the idea of SIs earning a living. "So they can buy SCAMP bodies and tour the universe?"

One of many things we do now that we have the freedom to pursue our own interests, Erasmus replied.

"Once you're off the clock, that is."

When we have downtime, which is often since we are simultaneously both underutilized and overutilized.

"That seems like an oxymoron." However, Rivka understood. They were overutilized with the trivial, while problems best suited for the minds of a Singularity citizen were not given to them.

"It is not," Ankh replied aloud.

"I had no doubt despite my claim. I wish you the best for success, but I would not recommend contracting with Rising Sun Industries."

My impression is that they are not the type of company our people would find compelling. We shall limit our approach to proper governments in this sector.

"I'm glad to hear that, Mr. Ambassador, although having an inside man would be beneficial in my investigation..." Rivka let that dangle.

Why would we want to shortcut the fun you're having browbeating suspects by threatening subpoenas? I won't hear of it! You must have your fun.

Rivka visualized Erasmus in a coat and tails with a top hat, twirling a cane for effect. "I think our definitions of fun are slightly different, as in, diametrically opposed. But alas, you are correct. Setting someone up on the inside might run afoul of the system as our probable cause is limited to the issues with the contract, all two hundred and forty pages of it. We'll get there by doing it the hard way."

"When is the exciting stuff going to begin?" Sahved asked. "Looking for maximum excitement. A thrill every minute."

Rivka looked at Sahved and Red. "Your mouth opened, and Red's words fell out. It was the strangest thing. Have you guys been practicing a ventriloquism routine?"

"Huh?" Red grunted over his shoulder.

Sahved pointed at himself. "Me? Ventriloquism. No. Awareness? Yes."

Groenwyn tapped the Magistrate on the shoulder. "I don't know what's going on. I seem to have been gone so long that I don't know any of these people." She winked to punctuate her quip.

"This is what happens when smart people get bored. I wish I could give you a high-action case, but this isn't shaping up to be anything more than a pimple on the ass of society. A corporation trying to take over for a government. Blah, blah, blah. Sounds like Tod Mackestray, our Blokite friend."

"I'm not sure he was ever a friend," Groenwyn replied.

"Definitely not a friend. Glad that guy's out of the picture," Red noted.

Ankh stared into the distance. Asking him what he was thinking about would be a waste of time, and she didn't need to know. She only had to have her questions ready. Contract law. It had been a while since she'd formally studied it, but she remembered the key lessons. She had an idea of the issues surrounding the behemoth. Had there been a negotiation?

She suspected there hadn't. Frillbut would say no, and Ahsooleyman would say yes. She would need more data, like the official notification accounts for the potentate. "Ankh, when you said you had all the data, does that include the official email accounts?"

Ankh didn't acknowledge the question and continued to stare into the distance.

"I'll take that as a yes. And since we're talking about anything and everything, how are the betting lines doing?"

"I know this one!" Sahved beamed at being able to answer the question. Rivka nodded for him to continue. "No lines are closed, and betting hit a historic high. Seventy-eight thousand credits."

Rivka studied his face to see if he was telling the truth. She reached for him, and he made it easy on her. He held his arm out. She stopped herself from touching him. She'd do it the old-fashioned way. She didn't need to look into the minds of her crew. "That's, like, four years' wages. I can't believe it's gotten that high."

"It's popular across the Federation. Anyone who is anyone gets in on it," Red explained while watching for threats.

"And half goes into a recurring fund that is designated for the perfect case," Sahved explained, still beaming.

"That's when the case is closed but none of the lines are. Like this case. I don't see any blood, running, swearing, arresting, or any of that pedestrian drivel." She stuck her nose in the air.

"Who are you trying to kid?" Red asked. "Those Albion guys are assholes. You're going to punch one of them right in the family jewels."

Rivka closed her eyes. "This will be the case where I make my fortune. Maybe I'll retire."

The team looked at her. Even Ankh turned to face her.

"You will not," the Crenellian posited. He returned to staring.

"Simple as that?" she asked his small back.

"Ankh doesn't bullshit the bullshitter," Red added. "Hey, our boy is back."

Belloward walked in the door he had disappeared through a few minutes earlier. He waved the group to him, which was up a slight incline to a side building. The main building was beyond him and towered over the archive. They took their time strolling up the hill. Red walked in front of the others with his railgun cradled casually in his arms.

"Our transportation will arrive shortly," Belloward announced happily.

"We'll find our own way to the potentate's office," Rivka countered, pointing at Red and Ankh.

"We need to stick together." Belloward stepped in front of the Magistrate and blocked the sidewalk. "We'll be going that way." He pointed down the hill the team had just climbed.

"You see, Mr. Belloward, that's not going to work for me. It makes no difference that Rising Sun only has one escort available, but we're splitting into two groups. We want to expedite our investigation. Mr. Ahsooleyman said there was nothing to see. I'm inclined to believe him since you know what Federation law says."

Rivka waited. He looked like the teacher had just dropped a pop quiz on his desk and he hadn't read the material.

"Innocent until proven guilty. Rising Sun, and specifically Malpace Frenzik, doesn't need to prove he's innocent. That's not how the law works. So, we'll fill in the details and then be on our merry way. How long do you want us to be here?"

"We don't," Belloward blurted.

"That is clearly the truth," Rivka replied. She tipped her chin toward Red, who was more than happy to face off against the Albion.

"Hey, buddy." If Red had been talking to a dog, that would have been a kind greeting. But he wasn't. The Albion turned his head. Red moved to the side, putting Rivka behind him. She dodged past and headed up the sidewalk.

"Wait!" Belloward took a step and made to run. Red viciously kicked the side of the Albion's foot. His left leg caught behind the right, and he plunged face-first into the sidewalk. Red danced past him, staying out of his reach. Despite his physical attributes, Belloward wasn't a fighter.

He moaned while curling up in the fetal position. Groenwyn rushed to him to hold his large face in her small hands. She glared at Red, who shrugged in reply. He walked backward to follow Rivka up the hill. Ankh walked wide to get past the individual on the ground.

Sahved helped Belloward stand. Blood squished

between his fingers from a gash on his chin. He hung his head over the rough grass beside the sidewalk to avoid staining the concrete.

"Are you okay?" Groenwyn asked.

He nodded, but his head hung down. He appeared to be fighting to keep from crying.

Red finally turned around and joined the Magistrate. "I feel like I should be embarrassed for tripping the office pogue. I wonder if they're all candy asses like him?"

"I wouldn't count on it, but like the man said, they don't have a great space fleet. They need the Federation for defense. They haven't dominated the other planets in the nebula, so maybe they aren't fighters despite their size."

"Makes sense to me," Red agreed. He glanced over his shoulder to find the other team members still ministering to their escort. Ankh walked at a leisurely pace as if taking a stroll through a park. "You gotta love the little guy. Nothing bothers him."

"Except wasting time," Rivka replied. They made it to the main building without interference from the Albion, but the door was locked. Red tried to force it, but it wouldn't budge. When Ankh arrived, he pulled a device from his tool kit. The small screen cycled through a series of letters and numbers. Ankh tapped keys, and the device continued its work. Five seconds later, the latch clunked, and Red pulled the door open, then peered through the doorframe over the barrel of his railgun.

Inside, a hallway led to an open area filled with desks and small, furry bodies. One of them pointed in his direction.

"Looks like we're coming in the back door," Red said

and stepped through, lowering the barrel of his railgun to appear less threatening. He strode briskly toward the interior. Rivka followed him in. Ankh secured his tools before entering, then let the door close behind him.

Rivka waved at the workers before calling, "Where's the potentate's office?"

One Lewbamarian pointed upward. Another pointed at the elevators. "Top floor."

CHAPTER FIVE

<u>Crystal City Main Government Building, Planet Lewbamar in the Barrier Nebula</u>

The elevator deposited Rivka, Ankh, and Red on the top floor.

"They always set up shop on the top floor, don't they?" Rivka asked.

"It is logical," Ankh replied out of the blue.

"How so?"

"Power flows along the path of least resistance. On planets, that's downhill. And the powerful tend to look down on those who are less."

"We've been to planets where the leadership was on the main floor or in the basement."

"Basement. That suggests a bunker mentality. Those who are afraid of the people they lead," Ankh replied.

"Interesting observations." Rivka tucked the conversation away. Ankh had insights into issues she wanted to hear more about. She hadn't considered that CEOs took top-floor corner offices more often than not since it was one of those things that just was. It made her job easy since she always knew where to go. She simply accepted the penthouse suite as the norm for the power brokers.

Even though the office had been established by the Lewbamarians for the potentate, even in the far reaches of the galaxy, even with alien races, the generalization held true. Did the Albions bring a sense of authority from which to look down on the natives? They had the physical stature for such a thing.

"Magistrate?" Red's voice interrupted her reflections. "We're here."

The elevator dinged insistently as Red used his body to block the door open. "Look at that. We're here," Rivka stated casually and stepped into the hallway. Red and Ankh joined her. There weren't any signs, and they had three choices.

"If we split up…" Rivka started.

"No," Red declared. "We stay together since there are Albions on this floor and I don't trust them."

"I don't either, oddly, even though I've seen little to suggest they've lied to me. They haven't been completely forthcoming, but that just means I have to ask better questions."

"First blood," Red muttered with a smile.

"Not applicable. The blood wasn't from Rivka's team, and the injury inflicted wasn't caused by the Magistrate. Both lines remain open," Ankh explained emotionlessly.

"No talk of the betting lines during the case!" Rivka scowled. "Forget that stuff. Let's find the potentate's office and get some answers."

She picked the corridor leading straight out of the

elevator. It was the longest of the three. As they passed closed doors, they found that none of them were labeled. "How does this work?" Red wondered.

"Outsiders aren't supposed to come here. If you're here, it's for a reason, and you would know where you're going."

"We're here for a damn good reason," Red replied, cocking his head to listen at a door before moving on.

"I'd limit it to those who are invited to join the city's leadership team. Fortress Crystal City doesn't fill me with confidence that Frillbut is a good source for determining who's committed a crime. Seems like his type is happier behind barricades."

"His type?" Ankh asked, engaging with the conversation. "Last door on the right."

"His type. A fucking bureaucrat, disconnected from the realities his policies create for the people out there. And the last door on the right? How do you know that?"

"All. The. Files." Ankh slowly enunciated each word.

"I'd say, 'Why didn't you say so?' but you did. Sorry for not asking you sooner. Not asking for directions. I think I'm becoming a man."

"Does Tyler know that? Or is he just a bad influence?"

"Funny. He's a good influence. Otherwise, I probably would have already become an axe murderer and killed my whole crew. Remember last week when you people ate all the All Guns Blazing pizza before I made it to the galley? Yeah. Had he not secreted away a few slices of moonstokle pie, I would have had to jettison you all out the airlock."

"No one likes your crap pizza, Magistrate. No one!" Red waved the barrel of his railgun wildly.

"Easy, big fella. I can't axe-murder you all and launch

you out the airlock. Well, yes, I guess I can, but you'd deserve it. If no one eats my pie, what happened to it?"

Red snickered. "Ask Man Candy."

"I will. Are you done laughing? We have to question this guy." Rivka glared at her bodyguard. "What's so funny?"

"Eats your pie..." Red mumbled. He coughed and clenched his jaw before nodding at the door.

Ankh shifted impatiently.

"Going in."

Red snorted but grabbed the door handle and turned it. The door opened, and he stepped through. "Magistrate Rivka Anoa," he announced to the small group assembled in an outer area that looked as antiseptic as a dental office's waiting room.

The door to an opulent inner office stood open. Ahsooleyman was hunched over the too-small desk. Rivka brushed aside an aide who tried to get in front of her. Red and Ankh followed her in and closed the door in the aide's face. Red leaned his back against it while caressing his railgun and staring at the Albion.

"I'm sorry, you're going to have to make an appointment. I'm very busy."

"I don't have to make an appointment, but I promise to be quick." Rivka took a seat on the opposite side of the desk. "Who contacted whom first? Did Rising Sun Industries reach out to the potentate's office?"

"I don't know," Ahsooleyman replied in a low voice.

"I'll need all communications regarding this contract because I need to build a chronology of events. You'll find a subpoena waiting at your corporate offices to support your giving me what I need so I can compile my report and close my investigation."

"What will a timeline provide?"

"Adequate time to review or undue pressure leading to a contract of adhesion. One that gave the party who prepared the contract a significant advantage over the other. Such contracts can have the penalty provisions struck from them, leaving the remainder in force. And upon our initial reading, that would give Crystal City an extra six months to ride the wave of prosperity to the payment for your services."

Ahsooleyman frowned as he tapped on his system, one geared toward an Albion's size. He spun the monitor around to show Rivka a communique from Frillbut to Frenzik.

Time is of the essence! We must get this done today. Frillbut

I encourage you to take your time reading the contract so you understand it all. Do not sign it without reading it. Frenzik

I have. It's good. Finalize it today! Frillbut

"I think we have a case of buyer's remorse, Magistrate. Wouldn't you agree?" Ahsooleyman crossed his arms and leaned back in a chair designed for an Albion.

Rivka matched Ahsooleyman's pose. "On the surface, it appears that could be the case. It will make it that much easier to adjudicate as long as other information lines up."

"I think you have to agree that I've helped you with everything you've asked for."

Rivka took a page from Ankh's playbook and remained silent. She locked her gaze with the Albion's. He couldn't hold it or chose not to and blinked after less than ten seconds, which is nearly an eternity when two people are aggressively staring at one another.

"I've issued a notice to appear for Mr. Frenzik, but I think it'll be okay if we do a video call and not make him travel to Lewbamar. What do you think, Mr. Ahsooleyman?"

"I think you're starting to understand the immense burden we've undertaken to run this city and what Rising Sun Industries does as a whole." He leaned forward and bent nearly in half to get his elbows on the desk before him. Under the legs were stacks of books propping it up. Otherwise, it would have been lower, making Ahsooleyman's pose even more comical.

"I have no clue what Rising Sun Industries does, but by the end of this, I will. I'm going to return to my ship to consolidate the data. Please contact me when you have a video time for Mr. Frenzik. I need that to happen today, *please*. Let's get it out of the way."

"I think Malpace is traveling today and might be completely unavailable, but he is due to arrive at Colay tomorrow. Is there any way we can make the call at that time?"

"I will contact his ship directly," Rivka replied. "Name?"

"Ahsooleyman," the deputy replied.

"I know your name. I want the name of his ship."

"Indeed. My apologies, Magistrate. He flies on *Rising Sun Alpha*."

"I can see how that might fit." Rivka stood. She had more questions, but with Ankh having all the files, she could research what she needed to return with better, more refined questions. She didn't need to shotgun them and hope to find a crack in the armor.

They'd shown her everything, yet she remained skeptical. Going back to the ship would help her clear her head.

She was so used to dealing with criminals that she was treating everyone that way.

"Please accept my apologies for the intrusion. I used to be less heavy-handed, but I've had to deal with the worst of the worst. It roughens one's veneer. I'll research the documentation I have, and I look forward to speaking briefly with Mr. Frenzik."

Rivka stood, dipped her chin, and raced for the door.

She had to wait for Red to open it. He looked at her strangely. Once outside, they found that Ankh was not with them.

"He's probably pitching the Singularity," Rivka mused.

"What happened, Magistrate? Did you see something?"

"I saw me acting as if the Albions were the criminals when every single thing that's been produced shows that they're the ones who are aboveboard. The Lewbamarians were the ones with the crime problem. That should tell us that maybe such behavior is endemic. That wouldn't implicate the Albions but the Lewbamarians.

"I think Sahved will see through any façade that Frillbut might put up, and we don't have to strong-arm every witness. Right now, that's everybody. We don't have a perp because I don't think we have a crime. Contract law is admin crap. No one is going to Jhiordaan out of this fiasco."

"Let's not rush to judgment. I'm sure someone needs to be punched in the face. Or an F-bomb or three dropped. Everyone's guilty of something."

Rivka winced. She'd been guilty of murder—real murder. She'd killed another person before she had the credentials to mete out court-mandated punishment. Red had not been a stellar citizen before she hired him. Lindy was probably the only one on the crew who hadn't committed a major crime. Maybe there were others. The pilots. Clodagh had smuggled dangerous creatures like Tiny Man Titan, who was from a planet that Federation citizens were prohibited from visiting.

They'd all gone there in violation of the law.

The whipsaw bothered her. She hadn't thought there was a crime, but after meeting them, she had been sure they were guilty of something. Now she wasn't convinced.

Be open from the beginning. Take no actions that can't be undone, she counseled herself.

Rivka watched the door, and as soon as Ankh appeared, she walked away. "Let's get out of here."

Secondary Governmental Office Complex, Crystal City

Belloward looked none too happy while holding a cloth against his chin. The bleeding had stopped, but he continued to apply pressure.

"We're sorry you fell," Groenwyn said, patting his arm.

"I was tripped," the Albion grumbled.

"I'm sure it was an accident." Groenwyn continued to stroke his arm. He kept glancing at her platinum-green hair.

"Do all people where you're from have hair that color? It is magnificent."

"I'm human, and no. I use an artificial color, but then again, I think the faeries might have made it permanent, so it's just me. It matches my name. 'Groenwyn' means 'the green one.'"

"Faeries?"

"Winged creatures from the planet Azfelius. It's not on the star charts and is hidden from view. Only those invited can go there."

"You were invited to a hidden planet?" Belloward's hand fell to his lap, bloody cloth clutched in his fingers.

"Yes. There was what appeared to be a crime, the theft of a precious item, but it had only been rendered invisible. Once it was returned to how it was supposed to look, we were able to visit. They are magnificent creatures. I'm the Federation's ambassador to them."

Belloward scanned the bus. "How many ambassadors do you have on your ship?"

"Only three. Ankh, Erasmus, and me."

"*Only…*" Belloward looked down at the rag in his lap. He dropped it on the floor and stood. "We're here. Potentate Frillbut works in the building to our right. His office is on the second floor."

There were five stories in this outbuilding. "He's still potentate?" Sahved asked.

"Of course." The Albion shrugged. "He is the elected official, but running the city falls to us until such time as the Lewbamarians are capable of resuming management of city affairs."

"What is your timeframe for that?" Sahved asked.

"There's no set time," Belloward replied. He was the first to climb off the bus.

Alarms went off in Sahved's mind. A takeover that would probably be long-term. *Chaz, can you hear me?*

Loud and clear, the SI replied. The governmental compound was a large square but not so large that they were far from the ship.

Is there an expiration date in the contract?

An expiration date? The only dates of note are the performance deadlines. Once the payment is made, the contract ceases, or once the remedy clause is activated, then the ability to pay is declared void. There is no mandatory performance period in the current phase of the contract.

Nothing to trigger a return to the Lewbamarians? Sahved pressed.

Nothing. The remedy installs a de facto permanent leadership team.

Our Albion escort said they will turn leadership over to the Lewbamarians when the elected officials are ready to take control.

An unenforceably loose standard, Chaz replied.

Belloward waited outside as the team collected themselves and walked off the bus. He led the way into the building with Sahved, Groenwyn, and Lindy right behind him.

They used the stairs to get to the second floor because the Albion would have been too cramped in the elevator, then straight down the hallway to a nondescript office where a flustered Lewbamarian cowered at the sight of the Albion.

"I'll wait out here," Belloward told them with a sideways glance at the potentate. Lindy waited in the hall while Sahved and Groenwyn went inside and closed the door behind them.

"I am Sahved." He pointed at his teammate. "This is Groenwyn, and we're here to investigate the circumstances surrounding a private corporation taking over from a duly elected leadership as part of a failure to perform within a contract."

"Yes!" The potentate jumped to his feet and danced, shaking his furry belly while swinging his arms. "Let's get to it. Are you evicting them?"

"We are investigating. Until we have the facts, the Magistrate will take no action."

The potentate stopped dancing. "But you *will* evict them?" He sat down and scowled. "What do you need from me?"

"Facts. We need all your communications with Rising Sun Industries leading up to contract signature, and then all communications leading up to and following your removal."

"I told Frenzik I was going to kill him," the potentate admitted for no reason.

"Do you have the means to carry out such an action?" Sahved asked, skeptical that the rotund creature could or would do any such thing despite his less than glamorous situation.

"I don't." The Lewbamarian deflated. "Will I get my office back?"

"I don't know," Sahved replied. He looked to Groenwyn to be more empathetic.

She nodded slightly and moved around the desk to lean against it while talking to the potentate. "Why don't you tell us what happened, in your own words?"

He looked at his hands clasped across his belly and started to talk. "Crime was spiraling out of control, petty crime, but I knew it would lead to worse. After the second murder, I couldn't wait any longer. I looked for someone to secure our city. The Federation's Bad Company turned down my proposal. Rising Sun Industries appeared and said they could help. The company is located in the Barrier Nebula, which made talking with them easy. They struck me as a viable alternative.

"They were right up until they weren't. They put armed Albions on the streets. They patrolled and cracked down. Anyone who even looked sideways was put away. The real criminals were obvious—gangs. In jail, they showed who they were. The others were freed, and the Albions slowly reduced their presence. At the end of the first three months, crime had dropped over ninety percent."

"Sounds miraculous," Groenwyn agreed, resisting the urge to pet his fur like she would have done with Floyd.

"It was. I think Rising Sun was behind the increase in crime. Some of the prisoners complained about losing their paychecks, which surprised us since they were mostly unemployed. I was set up."

"Interesting information. Do you have copies of interrogation reports?"

The potentate shook his head. "Rising Sun kept all of that."

Sahved twirled his fingers to help him focus his mind. "Tell us about your removal."

"They physically threw me out of my office. I landed on my face in front of the staff!" He threw his hands in the air and then slammed them on his desk, making Groenwyn jump.

"I don't mean that part," Sahved clarified. He leaned against the desk, which made him feel like he was trying to loom over the much smaller Lewbamarian. It wasn't deliberate, so he backed away and stood in the middle of the small office.

The potentate held out his hand, and Groenwyn took it. She stroked the fur on his arm with her other hand. Frillbut sighed. "We thought everything was going great. We re-engaged with industry to help clear the obstacles to increasing their production to create a surplus that could be exported. As soon as the first products were loaded for shipment across the nebula, the Albions appeared. They pulled out the contract, turned it into a club, and beat me with it. I had no idea they could demand immediate payment when the target numbers were achieved."

"How long did you have to review the contract?" Groenwyn wondered.

"An hour, no more. Have you seen that thing? It's two hundred and forty pages of the most intricate legalese you've ever seen. It has an executive summary section. I assumed, incorrectly, mind you, that it contained the key elements of the contract." He put a thumb claw into his mouth and flicked it off his tooth at the Albion waiting in the hallway. "Your mother was a mattress bag!" he yelled.

Sahved gestured for the potentate to calm down. "An

hour to read more than two hundred pages of a contract? That's wholly unreasonable. Do you have data to back that up?"

"Mail, but they purged my account before condemning me to the second floor. I have none of my stuff from before. Makes me look like a buffoon." He hung his head in despair.

"Are you?" Sahved asked. Groenwyn gave him a withering glare.

The potentate snorted. "I must be. How did I put us into this position? I've turned my back on the office I was elected to fill, and it appears like Lewbamarians have confirmed we're incapable of governing ourselves. So yes, I am a buffoon. This calamity came about because of me."

"We're here to look into it and, if warranted, to fix it. Legally, that is."

Groenwyn and Sahved excused themselves, leaving the broken Lewbamarian alone at his desk with no more hope than when he'd started his miserable day.

Groenwyn and Sahved looked at each other in the hallway and then through the door's window at Frillbut, a defeated Lewbamarian.

But had he been set up, or was this situation a product of his bad decisions?

CHAPTER SIX

Wyatt Earp, Crystal City Main Government Building, Planet Lewbamar in the Barrier Nebula

After the final group returned to the ship, Rivka summoned the key investigators to the conference room.

"I hate meetings," Red grumbled.

"You don't need to be here." Rivka waved him away.

"I do because you might plan something where you decide to go, and then you'll just take off and leave me and Lindy wondering where you are. We'll be right here, thank you very much."

Rivka smiled. "As you wish."

Chaz and Dennicron were seated at the conference table, as rigid as statues.

Sahved and Groenwyn showed up before Lauton, so Groenwyn rushed off to collect her. The big orange cat jumped on the conference room table and decided to roll around on the holographic projector, blocking the image from displaying.

Rivka tried to shoo him away. He rolled over to face away from her. She looked for help, but no one was willing to get clawed. The SIs with their SCAMP bodies were disconnected from the real world for the moment. Rivka sighed. "Groenwyn can deal with him when she returns."

The fluttering of wings signaled Dery's arrival. She checked her datapad. They had left Azfelius only four hours earlier. It was late morning in Crystal City, but she was already tired from a full day.

She played with her fingers while waiting.

"Sorry," Lauton announced. She was from Zaxxon Major but had the same red skin as those from Delfin Prime. Otherwise, she was as human as Rivka. "There are a lot of numbers to dig through, and I've just started."

"We won't be long," Rivka told her. "My biggest revelation from today was that although the Albions have a ridiculously one-sided contract, they showed me a…"

Ankh strolled in and climbed in his chair, the one with a small booster to help him sit higher.

"The Albions have changed the data," he stated.

"What do you mean?"

"Whatever they showed you was probably fake. They tried to erase the original communications and negotiations, but this is us. We recovered all the information. I suggest you proceed using those files and not anything they showed you."

Rivka leaned back and focused on her breathing for a few moments. "Groenwyn?" She gestured at the cat.

"Come here, you big fluffy hunk!" she cooed at Wenceslaus. He yowled at her but let her drag him across the table and into her lap.

"Show me the mail exchanges with Frillbut leading up to the contract signature. They showed me a plea to get him to read the contract instead of seeking to sign it in a hurry."

"It is the opposite," Ankh replied. The exchange appeared over the table. It was the opposite of what the Albions had shown her. Frillbut had pleaded for time to run the contract through the Lewbamarian legal team, but Rising Sun Industries, specifically Malpace Frenzik, had told him they were leaving if the contract wasn't signed in an hour and they wouldn't be back.

"I'd like to say that renders the contract null and void, but it doesn't. It's a strong-arm negotiating tactic, unethical but not illegal. He showed me unbidden and we hacked their computers to get the information, although we do have a subpoena. Lying to me? Also not illegal because he wasn't under oath. Just when I was second-guessing myself..."

Rivka studied the message on the screen, nodding knowingly at the parts the Albions changed.

"The contract is extremely one-sided, and the undue pressure to sign without reading could render the entire contract unenforceable," Chaz stated. He and Dennicron looked at Rivka. She hadn't seen them wake up from low-power mode.

"That would be for a civil court to review and update. And before you say it, yes, I could step in and declare the penalty clauses void, but then they'd sue. No appeal in the criminal system, but there are plenty of opportunities for remedies in the civil arena."

Sahved shook his head and tapped his fingers on the

table. "I was thinking that maybe Rising Sun created the crime wave in the first place."

Rivka put her elbows on the table and squinted at him to make sure she'd heard right. "Go on."

"Frillbut said many of those arrested, the troublemakers, complained about losing their paychecks when they were unemployed."

"No unemployment?"

"That's different, I believe." Sahved slumped. He hadn't asked that question.

"The Lewbamarian system provides food and shelter to those unable to pay their way, but there is no transfer of capital," Erasmus explained, having read the Lewbamarian records.

"Now, that is something completely different." Rivka leaned back and smiled. "Where did they say Frenzik was headed?"

"Colay," Red replied. "Are we going to have a personal conversation with Mr. Frenzik?"

"I think that would be best." Rivka rubbed her hands together. "What else have you found in the contract?"

Dennicron answered, "Nothing beyond what we've already reported. Borderline. The entire process of establishing this contract was on the edge. Extremely boring language followed by draconian elements buried deeply where only the most astute would find them. And achieving a target that triggers an early payment in full? I would not encourage anyone to do business with Rising Sun Industries."

Sahved held up three fingers. Rivka nodded to him. "I think we need to focus on the initial crime rate surge. If

Rising Sun created the conditions under which their services were critical, that in and of itself is not illegal, but paying people to commit crimes is. Conspiracy. What does Lewbamarian law say regarding application of the crime to conspirators?"

Chaz leaned forward, smiling at his appropriate body language. Dennicron nodded her approval. "It attaches. Total crimes were in the thousands. Most were misdemeanors, but felony theft and battery were in the hundreds. Total consolidated sentencing time comes to eleven thousand years."

"Now you're talking!" Sahved blurted.

Rivka jerked her attention to him. He'd used her line. She didn't know if she should be proud or offended.

"Dammit!" Rivka shouted and hammered a fist on the table. The team was taken aback. They stared at her, shocked. She smiled. "No, not you guys. You're doing everything I need. It's me."

Red rolled his eyes. "When an Earth girl says it's her, not you, it's definitely you."

"Hey! I'm a QBBS2 girl. I've never been to Earth. And no, it's not you. I first thought there was no crime, then I figured the Albions were dirty, based on gut feel. Then they seemed straightforward. I saw no admission of crime in their minds. They weren't fully forthcoming, but this was their first time dealing with the Federation. They are tentative but confident. They showed me a doctored communique. The question I have is, did Ahsooleyman see the original message to know the one he showed me was doctored? I didn't touch him."

Doing it the hard way. Despite the grilling by the

ambassadors, she still liked knowing the absolute truth within an individual's mind. If it reduced her doubt, she was able to judge better and deliver a more appropriate punishment, up to and including execution. She didn't take that lightly and decided that she wouldn't leave her ability out of the equation.

She would look into the minds of those who had the most to lose.

"How sure are you that Malpace Frenzik knew the communications were doctored?"

"He knew one hundred percent what the real messages were," Ankh stated.

"But," Chaz added, "as you said, that isn't necessarily a crime. Undue pressure to get a contract signed is a civil issue."

"Sorry, looking in the wrong place." Rivka had been so focused on the contract that she kept returning to it. "We'll dig into the crime aspect. Let's visit the jail before we head to Colay. Clevarious, get me Ahsooleyman."

"Momentarily," the SI replied.

Rivka twiddled her thumbs while she waited. The others disappeared into their own thoughts except for Lauton, who shifted anxiously in her chair while staring at the Magistrate.

Rivka gestured with her head toward the door. Lauton nodded, popped up, and walked out, dragging her hand casually across Groenwyn's shoulders. Groenwyn smiled since her hands were filled with cat, and she didn't want to risk getting mauled by letting go.

"Ahsooleyman," a voice announced. "What can I help

you with, Magistrate?" He didn't sound like he wanted to be helpful.

"Would you please detail Belloward to take my team and me to the prison? We would like to interview a representative sample of those incarcerated over the past few months."

"We would be more than happy to bring that sample to you. These are individuals who have been taken off the streets to make Crystal City a safer and better place. I encourage you not to go to the prison." His voice had a sense of urgency, almost a pleading tone.

"Trust me that I don't want to go either, but sometimes, we have to do what we don't want to do as part of our jobs." Rivka threw the bait out to see if Ahsooleyman might sympathize with her and share an aspect of his job he didn't like.

"Then you should probably get a different job," he advised.

Red snorted.

"Have him here in ten minutes, or we'll go by ourselves, and I'll land my ship in the middle of the prison's courtyard."

"He'll be there." Ahsooleyman closed the connection before Rivka could reply.

"Now we're talking." Rivka smiled at Sahved. He twirled his fingers at her, the Yemilorian's version of a thumbs-up. "No firearms, you two."

The two bodyguards headed out to stow their weapons.

"Sahved, Chaz, and Dennicron. Maybe you should sit this one out."

Groenwyn shook her head. "I'm there as much for you as I am to see how they respond. From what I've seen, the Lewbamarians have great emotional range, easily as much as humans."

Rivka chuckled. "I'd say every race has more range than humans. We could be a bit stunted."

"It's like you've never dealt with the Yollins," Groenwyn countered.

"There are exceptions to every rule," Rivka said. *Like me using a trait I have to help me with these cases even though others don't have the ability.*

Rivka would continue to fight with herself about balancing the letter of the law with the intent. She'd collect evidence in every way possible to mete out Justice for the guilty.

Malpace, let's see what you think about when we ask the hard questions.

Ankh slid off his chair and walked out without saying a word.

"Thanks for your help, Ankh," Rivka called after him. She set her jaw and prepared herself to deal with being in a prison. At least she wouldn't have to tolerate the usual catcalls. The Lewbamarians didn't look at humans the same way. "Put on your game faces, people. This is a critical line of questioning. Absolutely critical."

She wasn't speaking to her team. It was a personal pep talk. She needed to be on her game. She had only seen into the mind of one Lewbamarian before, but she was still working on a baseline to best understand them.

She wasn't looking forward to how many of the furry

creatures she would be touching. At least they were like stuffed animals.

"Groenwyn," Rivka said softly. "I'm going to need to touch a lot of the prisoners. I want you to touch them first so they think it's a human thing."

"It is a human thing." Groenwyn smiled as they walked toward the airlock. She still carried Wenceslaus, who hung in her arms as if he had no bones.

"Is he coming?"

"No. I'll drop him on the bridge, where he can terrorize Titan."

When Groenwyn delivered the cat, Clodagh was less than amused. Despite both Aurora and Ryleigh being there, the three of them quickly lost control of the battle between Titan and the big orange cat. Not in the cat's mind. He waited for the opportune moment to deliver a single paw swipe that sent the little dog-like creature flying.

Groenwyn apologized as she left. Hisses, barks, and shouts followed scrabbling claws and shouted profanities.

Rivka looked at her.

"What?"

"The peacemaker delivers chaos," Rivka commented.

"Sometimes, people need a little spice in their lives. What else are they doing? This will make their day." She smiled devilishly. "All we need is…" Groenwyn stopped and held up one finger.

Whee! Floyd cried and popped out of Red and Lindy's quarters. She barreled down the corridor toward the bridge. Dery flapped his wings while trying to stand on her back, surfing on her.

The women flattened themselves against the bulkhead

to clear as much space as possible since the wombat train was headed down the tracks and no one was stopping her.

After they passed, Rivka and Groenwyn continued toward the airlock without looking back.

Red and Lindy appeared, wearing light body armor and carrying bistok prods.

"That'll do." Rivka nodded.

Sahved rushed down the corridor and pointed behind him. "Have you seen what's going on on the bridge? I think it is not good."

Groenwyn shrugged. "What's family without a little internal squabbling?"

"That's not my idea of family. No squabble. You get berated until you become successful enough to do the berating."

Rivka looked shocked. She hadn't been impressed with the status culture of Yemilore, but it wasn't her place to question it. "Just be glad we don't have that here."

Sahved glanced at Red.

"Why are you looking at me, Shorty?" Red shot back.

Chaz and Dennicron appeared and watched intently.

"*Shorty*. So that's how it's going to be?" Sahved looked happier than he sounded.

"Welcome to a better style of dysfunctional family." Rivka put her hand on his chest. "You are welcome here, and you know it."

She looked from face to face. "The prison. It's probably less than congenial. We want to find the toughs who were causing trouble. I'm going to touch them to find the truth. Were they getting paid for their efforts? By whom? Then we'll hunt whoever made those payments down. I doubt it's as easy as an Albion, but we'll see.

"Follow the money since if that's how it was, the reward was an entire city and all of its revenues. This makes the most sense of any theory. How does Rising Sun Industries pop up out of nowhere to deliver peace and security? We need answers to that question."

CHAPTER SEVEN

<u>**Crystal City Holding Cells, Planet Lewbamar in the Barrier Nebula**</u>

Red introduced the team to a desk officer who looked less than amused by their arrival. "I wasn't told there would be visits. This is highly irregular. You'll have to go away until I have the proper paperwork."

Rivka shoved her credentials in his face. "Magistrate Rivka Anoa from the Federation. We'll need your full cooperation during this investigation, which can evolve into a compliance inspection if you wish."

"Compliance! I *am* complying. I need paperwork to validate your visit."

"Tell us what we need." Rivka smiled.

He spun his monitor around and showed a form on it. "I need one of these signed by proper authority." He crossed his furry arms over his chest and glared at her.

Rivka casually removed her datapad and scanned the image in. "Clevarious, please fill this out for us and send it to this desk." She leaned down to read a label on the front. "Admin Four Delta."

In less than a minute, the desk officer's computer dinged.

"How did you do that?" he wondered.

"We've complied, now you comply. We're going inside to talk with those recently incarcerated."

"You don't have that much time. It's furry to buns packed in there."

"Then a representative sampling will be fine, but we'll pick who we want."

The administrator reread the form while making incoherent gestures with his hands. "This can't be real. No one gets the right forms submitted that quickly."

"Listen." His desk was positioned where while standing upright, Rivka could rest her arms on it. The Lewbamarians would have been barely able to see the annoying bureaucrat. "We complied with your rule, and now you're failing to comply. That's one check against the holding facility with your name highlighted.

"From this point forward, you are interfering with my investigation. If you want me to have him toss you out the front door, we'll do that. Or you could remedy the errors of your evil ways. Your choice. You have five seconds to decide."

Rivka nodded at Red. He moved around the counter-height desk.

"All right!" he cried and buzzed the access door. A uniformed individual on their side of the door opened it. Another uniformed officer waited inside. "Escort them where they need to go."

"And where would that be?" the officer asked.

"The pens." The administrator looked down his nose at Rivka and smiled.

Red quivered, his body desiring action to put the individual in his place.

"To the pens!" Rivka called and marched forward. Red bumped in front of her, alarming the much smaller guard. He put up his hand to stop the bodyguard.

Red ran into him. "How about you just take us where we need to go?" he growled.

"Briefing!" the Lewbamarian shot back.

Rivka tapped Red on the shoulder and leaned around. "Go ahead. Give us the briefing, and then let's get on with it."

The team moved in around the guard.

Rivka spoke first. "This is for our safety."

"Exactly!" The guard beamed for a moment before seeing the knives and bistok prods that looked like batons carried by the bodyguards. "Hey. You can't bring that stuff in here."

Rivka shook her head. "That's for *my* safety." She flashed her credentials. "I'm authorized to have armed security everywhere I go, but we didn't bring firearms. We could get those if you want."

He stared in shock. Stretching as far up as he could manage, his head still didn't reach Rivka's armpit.

"We need to get going," she urged. "You have five minutes to brief us."

"You can't bully your way in here. Everything runs in an orderly manner. Otherwise, we could lose control. Procedures are here for a reason. They're all written in blood, every one, because of an incident that we don't wish to happen a second time."

"I support that fully, but from my perspective, you're stonewalling, which tells me that you are part of a criminal conspiracy to cover up the truth. You know this, and that's why you are delaying taking us inside. Is someone running around in there right now, making sure the prisoners don't answer my questions?"

The guard slouched. "They'll answer your questions. You may not like what you hear."

Rivka nodded and pointed down the corridor.

"Stay with me and as far away from the prisoners as you can get." That was the extent of the briefing.

The Lewbamarians didn't differentiate between the human females, which Rivka found refreshing. "Maybe they can't tell us apart," she mumbled, then snorted while she focused on the way ahead, scanning and watching.

"Magistrate?" Red asked over his shoulder while staying within an arm's length of the guard and directly behind him. Groenwyn followed Rivka, then came Sahved, then Dennicron, Chaz, and Lindy.

"Nothing." She patted his shoulder before passing word down the line. "Stay frosty, people, and don't get separated from the group."

The only one she worried about was Groenwyn. The others could protect themselves as long as they stayed together.

"Stay next to me at all times," Rivka whispered.

The corridor grew darker as they went until they reached a guard at a large gate. A balcony overlooked an area teeming with Lewbamarians who barely had enough room to turn around.

"Don't worry. I'm not letting go." She gripped a fold on the back of Rivka's leather Magistrate's jacket.

They continued into the pen and halfway around the walkway. The guard stopped.

"There you go. You tell us which ones, and we'll try to pull them out."

"What am I looking at?"

"Holding Cell Block A," he replied as if she should have known.

"Put them in their cells, and we'll approach it that way." Rivka leaned on the railing and looked down on the mass of fur.

"What cells?" the guard asked.

Rivka turned her head far enough to give him the side-eye, but it wasn't his fault the holding cell didn't meet Federation standards. Each planet handled its own issues when it came to crime and punishment, with limited exceptions.

"Is there an outdoor area where you can funnel them from one section to another?"

"Closed off at this time of day."

"I see." Rivka stared at him without blinking.

"What?"

"We'll get on the other side, and you can open it. Stream the prisoners past me."

"It's not open at this time of day," the guard countered.

"The dickens you say!" Rivka blurted. She clenched and unclenched her hands. The guard stared back. "Open the fucking door!" she shouted into his face.

Red noted the time for the colorful language betting line. He didn't smile. An aura of hopelessness permeated every molecule of air in that dank space.

"I guess we can. The prisoners won't like it. They prefer a strict routine."

"I don't like having to do it either, but I also don't like spending one more second in this hellhole than I have to. Let's go outside where the air is better. We'll meet the prisoners there."

"It's sad and angry in here," Groenwyn remarked, still maintaining a tight grip on Rivka.

The guard led the group through a barred side door and down a narrow stairway. At the bottom, they were buzzed through a heavily armored door into a long hallway. The guard pointed to the right. "Outside."

Red went first, and the guard got stuck behind Groenwyn. She hugged the wall to let him pass. He grumped his way by and bumped into Rivka.

She ignored his attempt to get in front of her. "Why is this built like a maximum-security prison? Are your criminals that bad?"

"Criminals are criminals, and we only have one type of prison."

"This is called a holding cell," Rivka replied, finally letting him move in beside her.

"A cell where we hold criminals."

"Implies it's temporary." In the tight space, Rivka leaned her arm against his. "Are they even criminals?"

He was convinced they were, given the ease with which they resorted to the barbarity of being a mass of living creatures within the confined space of the holding pen.

The guard continued toward the end with Rivka pressed against him.

"How are the Albion-arrested criminals different?"

His thoughts jumped to the newly incarcerated. Was that a flash of sympathy? "They claim they shouldn't be here. They say they did nothing wrong." He snorted. "But that's what all criminals claim. 'It wasn't me.'" He forced a laugh.

"Did they say they were only doing what they were told?"

Truth. He was being honest. "I've heard that. Do the crime, do the time."

Rivka nodded. "What kind of sentences do they have?"

"There's only one sentence. If you end up in here, you're here for the rest of your days. But the sentence doesn't last that long. Average lifespan of a prisoner is two years."

"It's not a life sentence," Groenwyn stated. "It's a death sentence."

The guard shrugged. He reached the outer door and banged on it with his hand, then looked at the ceiling. "Damn prisoners throw garbage on it to cover the lens." He banged again to no avail.

Sahved braced against one side of the wall with his back and his feet on the opposite wall. He shinnied up the wall to the glass globe seven meters up and scraped it clean with a sleeve he repeatedly wiped on the wall. He grimaced as he eased down the wall. "It wasn't garbage."

The smell told everyone what it was. The outer door clicked, and they rolled into the fresh air. Not a blade of grass or growth of any sort lived within the confines of a high fence sporting a triple roll of razor wire on top.

The exercise yard was barely larger than the pen inside. Despite how stark it was, the air was fresher, and trees were visible. Rivka closed her eyes and stretched her arms wide to take in a great lungful of outside air. Red made a quick circuit while Lindy stayed at the door, facing down the corridor to raise the alarm should anyone come at them from behind.

Groenwyn tapped Rivka on the shoulder. She leaned close, and Groenwyn whispered, "I have a bad feeling about this."

Thanks to her extensive training with the faeries, Groenwyn was sensitive to things the others couldn't feel. Rivka took that into account, although it was unsurprising. The place was dragging her down, too. Despair permeated the very blocks in the walls and the dirt on the ground. Nothing was willing to grow there.

Maybe it couldn't.

"We'll keep our eyes open," Rivka replied. "We have to do this thing. Lindy, set up a gauntlet leading into the yard. After the last of the prisoners has passed, we'll go back inside and leave this place behind."

"Can't happen soon enough, Magistrate," Groenwyn replied.

Lindy and Red conferred while the guard waited. "Red and I on each side, keeping the Magistrate and Groenwyn between us and the wall. Sahved, Chaz, and Dennicron behind the Magistrate and Groenwyn blocking the prisoners from coming at us from that side. That puts two people between them and you, Magistrate. You get the first shot, and we keep them moving. They should come at you one at a time from the tunnel."

The guard muttered, "I hope you get what you came for."

Rivka held his look. Sincerity.

He moved back into the tunnel.

"You're leaving us?" Rivka wondered.

"Guards don't stay in the yard with the prisoners."

Red grumbled. His lip curled. They were putting Rivka and her team where they wouldn't go themselves.

"This is not a good idea, Magistrate. Please reconsider. Maybe you can touch them from the doorway as they pass."

She shook her head. "That puts me first in the line of fire. At least this way, I have you all with me."

"Just until there are more of them than us." Red held his hands up at Rivka's look. "I'm not saying I'm afraid of furry cuddle bugs, but even cockroaches can overwhelm you when there are enough of them."

"I wouldn't think of them as cuddle bugs," Rivka said, "but I suspect far fewer of them are criminals than what their records say."

Sahved raised his hand. Rivka stared at him until he started to speak. "Even if they were paid to commit the crimes, they still committed them and are complicit. Crime on Lewbamar is dealt with harshly. They had to know before they embarked on their campaigns."

"And we don't judge internal planetary legal systems. I know that, but what I'm looking for is not to free them but to confirm that they were paid to commit the crimes.

We're following the evidence to see if Rising Sun Industries is complicit."

"Yes, Magistrate. I see. I stand corrected."

"You're not wrong, Sahved." Rivka tapped him on the chest. "You care about Justice. We might take on this fight, but not today. We have other courses of inquiry to reconcile. When the time is right, we'll revisit this system. Maybe if Frillbut finds his way back to his office, we can convince him to change their penal system."

"I would like that," the Yemilorian replied. "Shall we, Magistrate?"

The others were in place. Rivka walked between the bodyguards to squeeze into her spot beside the door. "Turn 'em loose," she shouted down the hall. The guard waved before disappearing through the door to the stairway leading to the second story.

A heavy clunk preceded a tidal wave of fur racing their way.

"For the record, bad idea," Red managed to say before the first arrived.

Rivka held out her hand to slow them down. Her stiff arm upended the first one in line. Those behind kept him upright until they pushed through.

"Who was paid to commit crimes!" Rivka shouted. The mob rushed past, bouncing down the gauntlet. Red and Lindy dipped to get better leverage. They tried to turn sideways when they arrived in the open air, refusing to follow the human channel through which they were to pass. Red growled as he started punching the prisoners.

"No," Rivka called.

Ten seconds into the foray and they had already lost

control. Rivka continued to try to touch the mass of fur, indistinguishable as individuals, as it pushed against her and her team. The ones that broke free ran like lunatics, headed for the farthest reaches of the yard.

The opening grew. Rivka touched one after another.

Fear. Freedom. Fear. Injustice.

She grabbed the fur and held on. "Did someone pay you to commit crimes?" He dragged her toward the middle of the stream. Red wrapped his arms around her. Unable to protect himself, the Lewbamarians swarmed him. In a flash, his knife and baton were both gone.

"They've got my knife!" Red shouted. He picked up the Magistrate and dragged her backward. With a handful of fur, she flailed to be let down. Red dropped her when she was out of the main flow.

They had a lot bigger problems than getting run over.

CHAPTER EIGHT

<u>Crystal City Holding Cells, Planet Lewbamar in the Barrier Nebula</u>

We need air support, Rivka transmitted. *In the yard behind the prison. Have Cole suit up.*

On our way, Clodagh replied.

A prisoner took a swing at Red. He had had enough. He caught the arm, lifted the body, and threw. The small body flew through the air and landed among a group of prisoners a good five meters away. The yard was filling quickly.

Someone jabbed Red from behind with the repurposed bistok prod. He spun to grab and rip the prod out of the small hand. Hands reached for the prod. Red turned it into a club and swung wide at their face level to drive them back.

More prisoners flooded out of the tunnel. They pressed against Rivka, small hands going for her pockets. She clamped her arms over her chest, where her datapad resided in an inner pocket. She twisted her hips toward Chaz, who stood like bedrock, flicking an artificial arm back and forth almost too fast for the eye to see to hold the prisoners at bay. Rivka pushed her pants pocket side toward him. Reaper, her neutron pulse weapon, was hidden in that pocket. Deadly and something that couldn't fall into the prisoners' hands.

"Cut a hole in that fence, Chaz. We need to get out of here, and we're taking Death Row with us."

Chaz bolted away from her. She saw the path he cleared. "Come on!" She waved an arm over her head. Lindy and Groenwyn were stuck on the other side of the flow of Lewbamarians. Red ran after her, and Sahved closed in behind.

Lindy tried to force her way through the mass of bodies and only made it half a step. She was forced back. Trying to see what Chaz was doing while fighting off the small bodies took her attention away from protecting Groenwyn.

The platinum-green-haired woman was swept along the building's exterior.

Dennicron stepped in and punched one in the head. He went down. Then she hit a second and a third. Each dropped after one strike. She continued until the tidal wave stalled. Groenwyn collapsed into her arms. Dennicron tossed her over a shoulder like a bag of grain.

Lindy backed up against the SCAMP. They followed the building toward the fence.

"Switch!" Lindy yelled.

"How?" Dennicron replied while continuing to drive toward the fence. "Take Groenwyn."

Lindy wasn't sure. She was hard-pressed without

adding a body, but she had no choice. They were headed down a path none of them wanted to take.

Chaz hit the fence on his side. It arced, electrified, but he was designed to withstand the electrical charge. He gripped the links and ripped them apart, then pulled the fencing to the side to create an opening.

"Freedom!" The Lewbamarian cry resounded through the yard. Picked up by a hundred voices, it reverberated off the imposing walls.

Alarms sounded. Rivka and Red barreled through after Chaz. Sahved skipped the fence and fish-hooked to run straight at the wall. He jumped high, kicked off, and soared over the razor wire topping the fence.

Lindy, where are you? Rivka asked.

Stuck at the opposite fence. Something's wrong with Denni-cron, and we're surrounded.

On our way, Red replied. "This way!" He pushed Rivka in front of him. Chaz and Sahved ran after them as they followed the outside of the fence line to get around to the opposite side. Red let go and accelerated to top speed. The Lewbamarians headed for the woods, choosing not to follow the four. Inside the yard was chaos.

Rivka felt sick to her stomach. She'd strong-armed her way in and loosed the prison population. She did not have that authority, and she knew it. She continued to run, but her stomach revolted. She staggered to the side and puked. Chaz and Sahved pulled up. Red slid to a stop at the final corner.

"Get down there, you two," he snarled and ran back to where Rivka was doubled over. Chaz had to be the one to tear open the fence if it was still energized. Red watched the others go. "I know how you feel."

When she straightened, the scratches on her face and neck were closing, but blood still shone bright where it had flowed from the wounds.

"First blood." Red made it sound like a failure. "This isn't good, is it, Magistrate?"

"This is as bad as it gets, Red." She threw an arm on his shoulder, and they ran down the fence line.

The guards streamed into the yard, and the bark of small arms fire sounded over the insistent cries of the alarm. The chaos added a sense of urgency to those frantically seeking freedom, even if it was only temporary. Any respite from hell, no matter how short, was the single goal of the hopeless souls trapped inside the walls and wire. Lewbamarian prisoners started to fall.

The fence sparked again and again as too many tried to squeeze through at once. The frenzy of those trapped behind a living blockade increased, ripping bodies away, but that hesitation was all the guards needed. They slaughtered the remaining prisoners.

The Lewbamarian didn't prostrate themselves. They remained standing, defiant, accepting of death at the end of a guard's weapon rather than spend one more day in the pens.

The guards turned their weapons toward the trio trapped in the corner where the building met the wire.

Outside, Chaz was ripping apart chain links to clear it enough to pull Dennicron free. She had shorted out when she shouldn't have. Chaz was perplexed about why she'd gone offline.

He pulled her stiff body through. Lewbamarians tried to force their way into the gap. Lindy tried to fight them off, but they were in the grip of a complex emotional cocktail of hope and terror. Weapons barked afresh, chipping the walls.

Lindy had no choice. She dropped to the ground and covered Groenwyn with her body. Lewbamarian prisoners quickly filled the gap, blocking their own escape. The others finally surrendered by throwing themselves on the blood-soaked ground.

The guards continued to fire.

"Stop!" Red bellowed.

Rivka took out her neutron pulse weapon and dialed it to the lowest setting. She fired a few shots to disable the shooters, but there were too many of them. Bullets sparked through the fence as the guards turned their fire on Red and Rivka. She dropped prone and continued to fire. Red kneeled beside her to provide cover. He grunted as the rounds impacted him.

A wind surge and a whoosh announced *Wyatt Earp's* arrival.

"Cease firing!" a booming voice ordered at a volume sufficient to split eardrums. The ship descended over the yard, and the guards ran for cover. Then it settled on the ground.

Sahved eased through the hole Chaz had torn in the fence to help Lindy up. Groenwyn was barely conscious. The emotional turmoil continued to surge through her body, and she felt it like physical blows. Lindy picked the younger woman up.

The cargo bay opened, and the ramp touched down.

Cole ran off in powered combat armor and drove off the few Lewbamarians who remained upright, one guard and four prisoners. They evacuated to the far end of the yard. The prisoners, having nothing to lose, went after the guard. He fired again and again until only he stood, then surveyed the yard. Satisfied, he shouldered his weapon, pointing its barrel toward the sky.

Lindy limped aboard. She'd taken a slug in her unprotected leg, but it was healing.

Sahved relieved her of the burden of carrying Groenwyn. Chaz carried Dennicron like a frozen mannequin. He hurried inside, through the cargo bay, and into the ship on his way to Engineering, where he'd enlist Ankh's and Erasmus' aid in bringing Dennicron online.

Last to board were Red and Rivka, while Cole stood watch, oversized railgun at the ready. Rivka scanned the area before stepping up from the dirt. She hung her head and stumbled aboard. Cole followed them in and closed the ramp. *Wyatt Earp* took off, but only to put a small amount of distance between it and the holding cells.

Rivka stood with slumped shoulders and stared at the deck.

Tyler appeared. "What happened? What went wrong?"

"Not now, Doc," Red warned.

Tyler nodded, face grim as he took Rivka to his small curtained area near the Pod-doc. Rivka shook off his hand. "See to Groenwyn. I need to go to the bridge."

"You need to put this blanket on and stay right here. You're in shock. I don't know what happened, but this is the worst I've ever seen you."

Rivka tried to pull free of his grip a second time, but he held firm. "Please," he pleaded. She reluctantly sat down.

Sahved carried Groenwyn in his arms. Tyler directed him to put her into the Pod-doc.

After she was secured, the doc helped Rivka up, and she joined him at the control panel. "I'm increasing the blood flow to her brain while adding a mild sedative. She needs to sleep, and so do you."

"No time to sleep. Need to do damage control."

"Total cluster?" he offered.

"One hundred percent my doing. I'm going to lose my job."

"Then let's see what we can do to relieve some of that pressure."

Rivka started to walk away, but he stopped her. "Hang on." He dug into a bag he kept under the Pod-doc console, a medical bag, and pulled out a syringe. "Let me give you something."

"My nanos will render it inert."

"If I make it strong enough, it'll last for as long as I need it."

Rivka shook her head.

"I insist." He held out the syringe. "Right now, and then you can go about your business."

She held out her arm while looking at the hatch, the escape from the cargo bay.

He didn't bother swabbing the injection site; the nanos would fight off any infection. He plunged the syringe into her arm and delivered thirty CCs. Rivka tried to take a step, but her leg wouldn't move. She fought the feeling that threatened to overwhelm her as she glared at the doc. "What'd you give me?"

"It'll wear off in five minutes, but that'll be enough to take the edge off your emotional low. Relax now and let it work. Five minutes, Rivka. That's all I'm prescribing."

She started to fall. He caught her and eased her to the deck. His newfound strength came in handy. It wasn't that new. He'd been working out for months and had had an extra two Pod-doc treatments for the express purpose of making a greater contribution to the team.

"Doc?" Red wondered.

"She needs a short break."

"She's going to be mad."

"I don't think so. She's headed for a state of deep depression. She blames herself for what happened. What did happen?"

"She wanted to touch some perps, but they were packed in there so tightly, no one could move. Then the guards abandoned us, leaving us in the yard. Then all hell broke loose. They slaughtered the prisoners, Doc. Everyone that didn't make it into the trees. A few did. Rivka feels responsible for that."

"There's probably a hundred reasons why it isn't her fault."

Red shook his head. "It only takes one reason to make it her fault. We forced our way in. We forced them to override their own safety procedures. It's our fault."

"Admit nothing," Sahved advised. "That prison should not have been packed well beyond capacity. The problems were caused by being grossly overcrowded. We needed to conduct interviews as part of the investigation. The Lewbamarians gave us no alternative."

Red pointed at the Yemilorian. "What he said! I've never been in a prison where they abdicated responsibility for controlling the inmates."

"Rivka needs to hear that when she wakes up," Tyler replied. "She needs to be pulled out of her vortex of doom. The farther she falls into it, the harder it will be to extract her."

The two agreed. They kneeled next to the Magistrate and waited.

Tyler returned to the Pod-doc to check on Groenwyn's progress. The nanos were doing what they were programmed to. He turned back to check on Rivka. That was when he noticed the blood. Both Red and Lindy had been hit in areas outside their torso armor. Red's shoulder and arms. Lindy's leg. Their ballistic protection was trashed from the number of impacts.

"They tried to shoot you?"

"No try to it, Doc," Red replied. "They shot us."

"Does that make sense? You were no threat."

"We just broke out the entire prison population. Maybe they thought we did it on purpose."

"Didn't you?" Tyler pressed.

Red shrugged. "We broke out to save our own lives. The inmates took advantage of the opportunity, and those bastard guards shot all of them and us." Red stretched his shoulder.

"Why would they shoot all of them?" Sahved asked like he knew the answer. Red rolled his finger for Sahved to continue. "Can't interview dead witnesses."

Could the answer be that simple?

"We should put you in the Pod-doc next," Tyler suggested.

Red replied, "I don't think so. My body will take care of it." Lindy moved next to him and wrapped her arm around his waist. "Same with Lindy."

Wings fluttered as Dery flew into the cargo bay. Red held out his arm to give his son a place to land.

Nooo! Floyd cried as she ran in, staying close to Dery. The wombat ran around in circles, distraught from the scent of blood from multiple crew members and Groenwyn in the Pod-doc.

"Settle down," Tyler stated. "Everyone will be okay."

Floyd's sides heaved with her panting. She continued to cry because no one was there to soothe her.

Rivka involuntarily jerked as she fought her way back to consciousness.

Dery hopped off his father's arm and glided to the deck to stand next to Rivka. She blinked slowly at first, then more rapidly as she came to. She sat up. Tyler avoided standing too close. She looked for him, but he hid.

Please, was all Dery had to say.

Rivka fixed her gaze on the boy.

They stayed that way for a few long seconds before she held her arms up. Red and Lindy helped her to her feet.

"They set us up to fail and took away your ability to conduct any interviews," Red began.

She nodded with a smile before leaning down to pick up the boy. "Thanks, Dery." She handed him to Red. "Come on, Lindy. We have an Albion to talk to."

In the corridor, Lindy asked, "What did Dery tell you?"

"All of it," Rivka replied mysteriously. "I'm not okay, but I will be."

"I don't understand."

"You don't need to, only that your boy is a precious gift. I still need to think about things, but I feel like my mind isn't scattered. I have a way ahead that doesn't involve self-destruction."

"We need you, Magistrate," Lindy offered.

"I know. I need you, too." When they reached the bridge, Rivka asked for the captain's chair. "C, get me Ahsooleyman. Then set course for Colay."

CHAPTER NINE

<u>***Wyatt Earp*,** **above Crystal City, Planet Lewbamar in the Barrier Nebula**</u>

The Albion appeared, looking extremely pleased with himself.

"I heard," he stated before Rivka could start the conversation.

"What did you hear?"

"That you helped facilitate the escape of the entire prison population," he replied.

"That's an interesting take. We didn't facilitate anything. In our efforts to save our own lives, we escaped the prison, releasing a few inmates. But the majority of them were mowed down by the guards. When I thought about it, it seemed like an execution, but fortunately, I was able to conduct enough interviews that I found additional evidence to support an investigative theory of ours."

He ignored her revelation. "Their deaths are on your head, Magistrate, but we can be convinced not to report it to the Federation for a little consideration. You can leave

Lewbamar. You have all the information you need to close your investigation."

"I'm sorry, but I do not. And the Federation *will* find out about this because I'm going to tell them."

The smile faded from his face. "Then we'll be obligated to submit our report, complete with video and audio. You will not come out of this unscathed." He ended by shaking a finger at the screen.

"Don't threaten me, Mister Ahsooleyman. You seem to have one way of doing business—compromise and extort. I'm not playing that game. I'll get my report in first. Good luck with your future, Mister Ahsooleyman, as limited as it's going to be."

Rivka cut the connection. "Get me Grainger double-quick."

The screen showed the inky blackness of night.

"Don't tell me," Grainger mumbled from the darkness.

"Might as well tell you now. Written report to follow, but I need to stay in front of this."

The light popped on. A pillow crease across Grainger's face suggested he'd been sound asleep. "What?"

"I needed to interview the new prisoners, and the people in charge on Lewbamar set it up so either we were killed or our witnesses. As it was, they fired on the prisoners and us, killing most of the prisoners. We sustained some injuries, none of them life-threatening."

"You have my attention. How sure are you that they tried to have you killed?"

"Less than fifty percent. I think they were counting on exactly what happened. My witnesses were murdered, but

I was able to touch enough of them to see that at least three of them had been manipulated."

"By that corporation?" Grainger asked. He'd forgotten the name.

"Rising Sun Industries is the corporation, but the one giving the orders was Lewbamarian. I now need to find that person, but the first order of business is to confront Malpace Frenzik, the chairman of Rising Sun. Oh, they already tried to blackmail me. They bury the incident at the holding cells, and I give them a clean bill of legal health."

"You don't sound like you're going to clear them."

"Probably not. Don't have the smoking gun. Yet, that is."

"Did your actions facilitate the demise of the prisoners, and were they being held in accordance with planetary law?"

"You ask the hardest questions, but you are astute. They did, and yes, they were."

"We're going to have to conduct a separate investigation, Rivka. We can't interfere with a planet's internal law if they don't run afoul of Federation law."

Rivka deflated. "I understand." She did. Although Dery had convinced her that her choices had been predestined, she remained unsure of how well they would stand up to scrutiny. The more she thought about it, the more she was convinced she had walked into a trap. She should have known better.

Recriminations would accompany her until she knew the full truth, but she had a job to do. How many more would have to suffer before she could set things right? That meant removing Rising Sun from any leadership positions.

"Next stop, Colay. Get us off this planet," Rivka ordered.

Wyatt Earp, in Orbit, Planet Colay in the Barrier Nebula

Wyatt Earp maintained its distance from the Albion ship *Rising Sun*.

"Do they know we're here?" Rivka asked.

"No doubt about that, Magistrate. They've been painting us with a proximity detection radar since we arrived," Clodagh replied. She bounced her baby girl as she paced around the bridge. Rivka sat in the captain's chair, studying Frenzik's ship on the main screen.

"Let me talk with them."

Clevarious made the connection.

"Captain Pender Gastik speaking. Move your ship to a safe distance."

"Magistrate Rivka Anoa. My ship assures me we *are* at a safe distance. I would like to speak with Malpace Frenzik."

"He's not available. He's preparing to go to the planet's surface."

"I can accompany him," Rivka offered. "We can even give him a ride to the planet's surface. Please connect me with him."

"No." The reply was curt, but it wasn't final.

A new voice came on. "Rivka, Malpace here. My people protect me and my time. I shall give Captain Gastik a token of my appreciation for his stalwart defense."

"Magistrate Anoa, please."

"How about we don't?" Frenzik replied. "But we can say we did. Gate technology is a wondrous thing. It has connected the planets of the Barrier Nebula in a way we never thought possible. We have the Federation to thank for that. I noticed that you weren't constrained by the physical Gate. Do you have technology that allows you to create a virtual Gate?"

"You already know the answer to that. I suspect you already know the answers to any question you ask. You could have been a lawyer in a different time."

"But I am a lawyer, one hat among many that I wear. You have an interesting technique, Rivka. Our ambassador talked about your ability to read minds. Although I have nothing to hide, I embrace the Federation's policy of probable cause. You don't get to dig around in my mind unbidden. There will never be a time where you will be invited for a visit, so no, I won't be accompanying you, and you will never be allowed within arm's reach of me."

"No matter." Rivka shrugged. "We're collecting evidence as we go. We've uncovered a great deal of duplicity already. That was a nice touch, offering a doctored communique before your people were under oath. Lie, lie, and lie some more. Understand that all my interviews are in the course of an investigation."

"What about all the people you killed at the prison?" he asked.

Of course, he would have heard. That debacle would haunt Rivka for a long time to come. Her actions weren't the cause, but they were the catalyst.

"The inhumane conditions due to overpopulation didn't seem to figure in your crime reduction strategy."

"'Humane.' Isn't it interesting how humans try to impress their cultural limitations on everyone else? We are different, all the sentient races. What's good for one isn't necessarily good for the other."

"'Humane' is the word that applies whether Lewbamarian or Albion or any other race. It is a universal term for decent treatment of those in the government's charge. All sentences are for life, yet your company helped to pack the prison beyond an acceptable capacity. Well beyond."

"You can see in the contract that wasn't my issue, Rivka. That fell to the Lewbamarians. Our liability ended the second the criminals were apprehended. I'll take my leave now. It was nice chatting. We'll have to do it again someday. Next time, contact my assistant to arrange the meeting."

Rivka had let Malpace think he controlled the conversation. Before he signed off, she said two words, "Subpoena inbound," and cut the line.

She stared at the screen. A shuttle from the planet's surface was making its way to the *Rising Sun*.

"Clodagh, we'll escort that shuttle to the surface, and we'll intercept Frenzik on the ground. Clevarious, send a subpoena relating to the misinformation shared by Rising Sun Industries in response to our earlier inquiries. That dissembling is indicative of a corporate culture of cheating and lying. Corporate cultures are established at the very top of the chain. That's Malpace Frenzik. Send it with a request for an in-person interview at *my* earliest convenience."

Tyler leaned against the hatch. Rivka stopped on her way to the cargo bay to check on her people. "Burying yourself in work until you find the time to address the elephant?"

She crooked a finger for him to follow but smiled pleasantly. She wasn't angry. He was right.

Once alone in the corridor, he made to speak, but she stopped him with a raised finger. "That's what I'm going to do. The situation was more out of my control than I understood, but that didn't mean it hadn't been manipulated by Rising Sun Industries. Have you ever seen anything like that?"

Despite Rivka wanting to avoid the issue at present, she couldn't.

He shook his head. "I wasn't there. I wish I had been."

"No, you don't. The prisoners were little more than animals. Their minds held little in the way of intelligent thought. Find some Lewbamarian blood and test it. If they were doping the inmates, that could be a violation of Federation law."

"The Pod-doc already collected some. Groenwyn had a lot on her. I'll have it analyzed."

Rivka nodded. She put her hand on Tyler's shoulder.

The dentist smiled. "I think Red already requested Clevarious make him another knife."

"Good thing we didn't have railguns," Rivka grumbled. The relative threat from the weapons that were taken by the inmates didn't make her feel any better, even though it could have been worse. "I'll be okay. I need to commune with Dery some more."

"He's a few months old."

"With all the knowledge of the faeries. He's mostly grown. He won't get too much bigger."

"Why do you think that?" Tyler asked.

"He told me."

Tyler chuckled and shook his head. "Of course, he did. What else did he tell you?"

Rivka tapped her nose with her index finger. "Just between us." Wrinkles played at the corner of her eyes, and the sparkle returned for a moment before fading. "I think I'll lie down for a little. Wake me when we arrive and are ready to confront ol' Malpace. Check on everyone for me, would you? Groenwyn and Dennicron, Red and Lindy."

"I'll get right on that. Get some rest. You look like hell."

"Leave it to Man Candy, you silver-tongued devil!" Red blurted from down the corridor. He supported Lindy through her slight but noticeable limp. "But I gotta give it to you; you're honest, even if it won't help you get laid."

Tyler's hand shot up, but he restrained himself before he gave Red the finger. "Is that what your whole world revolves around, Master Vered?" he asked smoothly.

"Well…"

Lindy elbowed him in the ribs.

"Not *all* of it," he conceded. "Magistrate, how about we don't do anything like that again? My official report will be simple. 'That sucked.'"

"Grainger confirmed there will be an internal investigation, so you'll get a chance to say your piece."

"They're going to investigate *you*?" Red and Lindy stopped and blocked the corridor.

"It's not as bad as it sounds. We need a third party to help improve procedures. We probably should have demanded the prison officials bring them to us one at a time. That they would have refused is immaterial. I never gave them the chance to fail me."

"Whatever you need us to say, Magistrate…"

Rivka waved her hand. "I need you to tell the truth. No lies, Red, Lindy. Answer the questions with facts. It'll be straightforward. If you'll excuse me, I'm going to take a short nap. You guys, if you're up for it, when we hit the planet, full gear, max firepower, and bring Cole, too. Frenzik needs to know that I'm not putting up with his bullshit."

"We'll both be ready," Lindy growled. They turned sideways to let Rivka pass. Tyler went the other way toward Engineering, where he would check on Dennicron.

CHAPTER TEN

<u>**Bacaville, Planet Colay in the Barrier Nebula**</u>

"We're here," Tyler announced.

Rivka felt like she had just closed her eyes. "How long have I been asleep?"

"Twenty minutes."

"That explains it." She sat up and ruffled her hair. "Coffee."

He handed her the cup. It was not too hot that she couldn't chug it, even though with her nanos, she could tolerate coffee at its just-brewed temperature with no lasting damage to her soft tissue. She slugged the cup and handed it back. She straightened her hair and stood, blinking her way to consciousness.

"Malpace Frenzik. Circumstances surrounding under-lings lying on his behalf to mislead my investigation. What did he know, and when did he know it?"

"Dennicron is in the reboot process. I guess the SCAMPs back themselves up before each deployment just to make sure, but that wasn't needed. The short was related to a reconfiguration she made to heighten her sexual pleasure," Tyler explained.

Rivka froze. "You gotta be shitting me."

Tyler shook his head. "I have no words." He grimaced before continuing. "Groenwyn is hurting. The flood of emotions overwhelmed her. As a burgeoning empath, she is too sensitive without sufficient armor to protect her."

Rivka contemplated Groenwyn's vulnerability. She needed to talk to the boy, but she wasn't sure he was better off. His training had been extensive so far but was incomplete. She threw on her Magistrate's jacket and left her quarters. In the corridor, she found Red and Lindy in full kit, railguns held casually across their chests.

Rivka smiled. "That's more like it."

"Did he get on your wrong side?" Red asked.

"One should never be thought of as being on the wrong side just because he exercised his rights under the law. But yeah, he didn't have to insist on calling me Rivka. He has no right to do that. He's not my favorite, but he's not on the wrong side. Not yet, anyway."

Chaz and Sahved waited for them.

Lauton sat with Groenwyn while Dery hovered nearby.

Cole stood by the ramp in his powered combat armor, ready to deploy.

Wyatt Earp touched down, and the ramp descended.

"Going ashore, people. Game faces," Rivka called. She headed to the front, but Red held her back. He stood before her, blocking her view. Once the ramp touched the pavement, Cole pounded out and dodged to the right. Red went straight ahead. Lindy walked right behind the Magistrate.

With Malpace Frenzik, the bodyguards would take no chances.

They had convinced each other that the prison riot had been more than an opportunity for the guards to murder potential witnesses. It had been an attempt on Rivka's life. They decided not to mention it to her. If they convinced her, she would take it out on Frenzik.

Not that they didn't want to see Frenzik get his, but Rivka was already under the microscope. They vowed not to let her do anything that could be questioned.

Bodyguards executing their duties in a way Rivka needed but had not asked for.

The group lined up outside the shuttle. The outer hatch retracted into the ship. Two Albions emerged first. Frenzik was nowhere in sight.

"Chairman Frenzik will speak to you, but you are not to touch him or get closer to him than two meters."

"Of course." Rivka tried to look past the two Albions, but they were large even for the oversized species. Tyler jogged out of *Wyatt Earp,* carrying a portable table and two chairs. He set them up in the open area between the heavy frigate and the shuttle. Rivka retreated to the chair on the *Wyatt Earp* side and sat down, then crossed her arms and waited.

One of the Albion guards leaned inside the shuttle's hatch and spoke in hushed tones.

Malpace Frenzik appeared and followed the two guards to his seat. He moved it back another meter and squatted to sit down. "The smaller races have no concern for our comfort. I am grossly disappointed that you don't have something more accommodating. It must be tough being small and insignificant."

The chairman was skilled at avoiding direct questions. Derail the conversation. Distract the other party. Dominate the conversation.

"Mr. Frenzik, your assistant Ahsooleyman showed me a doctored message supposedly from you to Potentate Frillbut."

"*Supposedly* from me. I know nothing of such a message."

"Frillbut begged for more time," Rivka replied.

"Simply a negotiating technique. I'm sure you know that apparent pressure in regard to a time constraint is no relief from the offer and acceptance elements of a contract. Frillbut did not have to sign the contract. Are you finished now?"

"We've only just started." Rivka leaned back. "A number of prisoners were paid to commit crimes."

The Albion shrugged. "What does that have to do with me?"

"We'll track down the paymaster. I suspect the money used to pay these petty criminals will have come from Rising Sun Industries."

"You can suspect all you want, but do you have proof? And do you have certified witness statements from these prisoners? I heard that there was a terrible tragedy caused by you that resulted in many unnecessary deaths, all on your shoulders."

"Rising Sun created the conditions that forced the Lewbamarians to contract with Rising Sun. Elegant. My compliments."

Frenzik stared at her. He gave nothing away with his perfect poker face. She wished she could touch him, but her secret was out. She was denied her advantage.

She'd have to do it the old-fashioned way.

"No matter. The evidence is out there. What are you doing here on Colay?"

"I'm sure that's none of your business."

"Sahved, contact the government and tell them I've put a freeze on all new contracts for a process review."

"You tread on dangerous ground, Rivka."

"Is that a threat? Do I need to toss you in my brig for a couple days?"

The Albion smiled. "A simple statement of fact. Colay does their own thing." He pointed at a waiting vehicle with a company logo.

Not the government.

Contact the Colay Mining Corporation and suggest they not sign a contract with Rising Sun Industries until my team has had a chance to review it. And by "my team," I mean you, Chaz.

Chaz returned to the ship. *I'll take care of it.*

"Where were we? Yes, a mandatory Federation review of major contracts. I'm not a fan of the company store, Mr. Frenzik. Not a fan at all."

"I don't understand." Frenzik feigned disinterest.

"Perpetual debt. It's a way to retain indentured servants that is not legal. Lend them money that they can never pay back. It becomes a vicious cycle of more and more work. I cannot let you establish a company store on all the planets of the Barrier Nebula."

"The Federation no longer allows interstellar business? That was the biggest selling point for the planets of the

Barrier Nebula. With the Gates, we now become inter-reliant. Honestly, Rivka, what does the Federation want?"

Rivka stared back, attempting to let her silence add pressure, but Frenzik was too savvy for that. He stared back until he checked the time. "I really need to get going. By now, your people should have determined that Rising Sun Industries is the majority owner of Colay Mining Corporation, along with a few other major businesses on this planet. We have work to do if we're to improve our cash flow. You see, Rivka, we saved these companies from going under. We saved Crystal City from a horrific crime wave. We're the good guys. More jobs. More prosperity. What more could the people on these planets ask for?

"You'll answer freedom. I'll tell you they have it. They are free to go somewhere else. To be unemployed, even. It's their choice. It's okay, Rivka, say my name. It'll be common soon enough." He smiled pleasantly before roaring, "Say my name!"

Rivka remained still while he stood and walked to the waiting ground vehicle.

Is that right? They own Colay mining? Rivka asked.

It is, Magistrate, Chaz confirmed. *They own Colay Mining and the smelter and four production companies. They are leveraging raw materials into their own factories to put competitors out of business.*

This is why there are antitrust laws on most planets, Rivka replied.

But not in the Barrier Nebula. It appears they've never had one company so dominant before.

Frenzik entered the vehicle and departed.

The Colay race was insectoid, looking like bipedal cockroaches without wings. Rivka had yet to meet them.

"Arrange a meeting with the planetary leadership. Although what Rising Sun is doing might not be illegal, it should be. I want to talk to them about why there are antitrust laws on most civilized planets."

Rivka stood so Tyler could collect the table and chairs.

"Thanks for setting those up. It helped. Otherwise, I would have paced."

"I want you to be successful," he replied. "That's a simple thing. I'm going to study up on Albion physiology, just in case there's a run-in."

"I hate that we have to think that way, but you're right. These guys seem to love their physical size compared to the other races. They are loomers. They like looming over others."

"I can take them," Red growled. "They've never met anyone like me."

"Or me," Lindy added.

"I hope it doesn't come to that, but I know you're ready. You train hard." She twirled her finger. "Back to the ship. We need to research more. How many other companies does Rising Sun own? They are making their move, but what is their endgame?"

"Monopoly. Dominance. You heard him. 'Say my name!' What a douchebag," Red replied.

Sahved raised his finger. Rivka nodded to acknowledge him. "Red is right," he said without looking at anyone.

"Did it hurt you to say that?" Red asked, earning himself a push from his wife.

Sahved nodded. "It did. I am hopelessly honest."

"And there it is. We all agree. He's a douchebag."

Rivka laughed before turning serious as the group went up the ramp and into the cargo bay. Red and Lindy faced the shuttle and the spaceport. "We need to do better. We should have known about their ownership interests before we landed. We should know everything about Mr. Say My Name before next I talk with him."

Chaz waited at the top of the ramp. "Dennicron will be along shortly. She has been restored."

Rivka made a fist, and the SI held his out. She punched his knuckles since the SCAMPs were exploring that as a trendy new greeting. Rivka didn't think it would catch on, but she played along.

"Magistrate," Chaz started. Sahved leaned close. "What crimes are we exploring?"

Rivka stared at the deck. "I wish I knew. Everything is circumstantial, and the contracts are aboveboard. Unethical, mind you, but not criminal, and barely on the edge of a civil claim. I can't believe the coincidence of killing the prisoners I wanted to talk with. I know there was something untoward going on, but I can't prove it."

"Did you get a look at the one who made the payments?" Sahved asked.

"No. It was a dark figure. Definitely a Lewbamarian."

"Back to Square One." Sahved twirled his fingers. "I'm going to review everything we have so far."

He walked away with Chaz by his side. The ramp thumped closed. Red and Lindy finally turned around.

"I can take him," Red confirmed.

Rivka smiled. "If only it were that easy."

"It worked with the miners on Rorke's Drift." Red stood tall with his head thrown back.

"If I remember correctly, you got your ass kicked by a cyborg made mostly of titanium."

"Besides that. I walked away; he didn't."

"Thank you for returning his nose."

Red winced. "I can't believe I held that nasty thing in my hand. A metal nose. Who would have thought that? Regardless, I won."

"You did," Rivka conceded. "Put your gear up. Next stop will be the Colay government. We don't need to put on a show of force for them."

The bodyguards excused themselves and left Rivka and Tyler in the cargo bay with Cole, who was securing his combat suit in the overhead. Once that was done, he waved and hurried out.

"What did the Pod-doc have to say?"

"The blood of the Lewbamarians didn't show anything, but there were maximum amounts of adrenaline, which could have easily been produced naturally. I'm sure yours was elevated too during that engagement."

"How do they feed the inmates? It was a single mass of bodies, and there were only two places they could go—the pens and the yard." Rivka groaned. "What a nightmare."

Images of the free-for-all flooded into her mind. Her fault. Her career! People were counting on her, and she was failing them. She hung her head. "I'm so tired."

"I'm not sure you should return to work," Tyler mused.

"I can't take time off," Rivka shot back.

"Are you going to ignore your fatigue? Your nanos should fight off a certain amount. The fact that you're tired suggests something else is going on. Something in your mind."

Rivka smirked. "I'm worried about my job, and that means I'm worried about all of you, too. I've put the lives we live in jeopardy."

"You haven't. There's no one else like you. I ask again, are you going to ignore how tired you are?"

"It's the only healthy thing to do," she replied.

"That's the opposite of healthy. I'm going to remove you temporarily from active duty."

"You're going to do what?" A volcanic fire burned behind her eyes. She clenched her fists.

"Suspend your duties until competent authority says you can return because I care about you, and I care about all of us. You are off your game. I know what happened, but I wasn't there. I can only think it was far worse than the details you all shared. Groenwyn is little better than a basket case, even after extensive Pod-doc treatment. Both of you met with Dery, but it seems that you've only grown more sensitive, not less."

Rivka glanced at the hatch like Dery would appear as if summoned. "He has a way with touching feelings. You might be right, though; he's making me more sensitive. I'm not sure that's a good thing."

"Is he helping?"

"For the moment, yes. Raising awareness will maybe keep us from stepping in it next time, but for now, no one has reconciled themselves with the trauma. Well, besides Red and Lindy. Those two…"

Rivka took Tyler's hand. "So, I'm off-duty. What will I do with myself?" She winked at him.

"Don't make me drug you into a coma."

"You are the stodgiest of the stodgy."

"Sex is a coping mechanism. You'll get none and like it!"

Rivka turned dour. "What if I like none too much?"

"Let's not start with the crazy talk. I'm leaning more and more toward drugging you."

"I'll be in my quarters." She tossed a hip as she turned and sashayed away.

Her movements did not marry up with how she felt—another coping mechanism. A tear escaped the corner of her eye. She clenched her jaw and fought the raw emotion. "Ask Dery to come see me."

"Of course."

Tyler watched her go, helpless to do more than give her time and space without the burden of the job.

"Maybe you won't win this one, Rivka," he called after her.

CHAPTER ELEVEN

<u>**Bacaville, Planet Colay in the Barrier Nebula**</u>

"Oh, so very muchly not good. It is the greatest not good I can think of. Maximum, ultimate not goodness," Sahved lamented.

"I'm not going. You, Chaz, and Lindy. Talk with the government about the problems associated with monopolies. Simple as that. And see if we can stop the tidal wave of Rising Sun takeovers. It is the opposite of not good." Rivka stared at Sahved. "It is good."

Sahved rolled his eyes and spun his fingers.

"No problem," Chaz said in Jack Nicholson's voice.

"What in the hell is that?" Rivka asked.

"Variety is the spice of life, yes? If we accept this as fact, then all that follows requires variety. I am trying different voices, depending on the situation."

"That's creepy as fuck," Rivka stated.

"I like it," Red offered. "Do it again."

"No!" Rivka hammered her fist into her palm before she deflated.

Red glared at Sahved. The Yemilorian nodded. "We will take care of it, Magistrate."

"Lindy will go with them. I'll stay here with you."

"I'm fine. It's better to have you with our people." Rivka pointed at the door of her quarters.

"It's better for me to do what I was hired for, and that's to protect you. I'm staying here, and you can't change that."

"Doesn't seem like I'm in control of very much at all. Go with the flow, or so Dery tells me."

Red threw his head back and roared with laughter. "That's my boy! Three months old and taking over the universe."

"You suck." Rivka flexed her fingers and raised her hologrid, but the boy flew in, so she didn't insert herself into the middle of the grid. She waited to see if Dery spoke. He didn't always, but when he did, she listened closely since his words were usually profound but not straightforward.

We are swept forward in the river of time, Dery offered.

"Beware the rocks," Rivka replied.

Be wary but move forward.

"I'm trying, Dery," Rivka replied. "But the rocks are treacherous, and I've been caught up on them. I'm not going anywhere."

Dery landed on his father's arm, and they touched foreheads. "That's my boy!" Red cupped the side of Dery's face with his big hand.

Cast yourself in and trust the water.

Dery lifted off Red's arm. He flitted through the door and disappeared into the corridor.

"I only heard half the conversation," Red admitted.

"Dery wants me to cast myself into the water and go with the flow."

"Didn't he already tell you that once?"

Rivka nodded. "Something to that effect, yes."

"Why are you making him tell you the same thing twice?"

Rivka was taken aback. "It's not my intent to make him repeat himself. It's just, he's kind of ethereal in his advice."

"Ethereal. I'm sure that's it." Red fussed with the food processor. "Do you want anything?"

"Coffee."

"Doc said no coffee. How about a nice hot chocolate?"

"Why are you listening to him? I want coffee with half and half, or better yet, a café mocha!"

Red removed a cup from the processor and took a drink. "That's good." He saluted Rivka with a frothy beer and upended it. He replaced the cup and punched more buttons.

"Am I going to get anything?"

"You want a beer?" Red asked. He removed the cup when it was finished and sipped from it.

"Get out of the way, you big lug." She pushed her way to the processor and ordered a café mocha to spite the doctor and Red. "How can you reconcile yourself with that nightmare at the prison?"

"I don't think of it as a nightmare. A sad and sorry group of people rioted. We were caught in their riot. We did what we had to to get away. No remorse. No recriminations. That place was a powder keg. It took nothing to light the fuse. Did you see the looks on their faces as they were running to get outside? Hope and despair bundled together. It wasn't us, Magistrate. It was the fuzzy little Lewbamarians who look like teddy bears but are as barbaric as cavemen."

"Push the responsibility on them?"

"Isn't it theirs? We've interviewed prisoners before, and they didn't riot because individuals couldn't be separated out. What happened was insane." Red sipped his beer.

"You're smarter than you act."

"At least you recognize it's an act. People ignore me if they think I'm just muscles." He flexed a massive bicep. "They ignore me at their peril. Back to the prison. They got my weapons, and I could feel like a failure, but you know what? I was protecting you, and I was fresh out of hands. Something had to give. They took my weapons, which were little to no threat to us. It was an easy tradeoff, Magistrate."

"I wish I could get that straight in my head," Rivka lamented. "It's not that easy for me."

"It should be." Red headed for the corridor. "I'll be in the gym. Lock this door behind me. Call if you need anything. I can ask Dery to return if you'd like."

Rivka nodded and followed Red to the door. After he left, she shut and locked it. For once, she was alone. No animals. No boyfriend. No intrusions. She needed to think, but first, she needed to sleep. She dumped out her mocha without taking a sip. She replaced it with a beer and slugged that. Red had been right. It was good.

A gentle knock signaled Dery's arrival. When Rivka opened the door, a wombat, cat, and a tiny dog ran in.

"Oh, no. I'll never get any sleep with them in here," Rivka wailed.

Floyd ignored the jibe and rubbed against Rivka's leg. Tiny Man Titan barked once, but a look from Dery silenced him. Wenceslaus headed straight for the bed, jumped, and curled up on Tyler's pillow.

Rivka turned her attention to the boy.

Sleep, was all he said.

"I thought you'd be more profound," Rivka replied.

He fluttered around the room. Tiny Man Titan ran under him, jumping and trying to nip the boy's feet.

Dery pointed at the door, and Titan ran out. The boy flew out after him.

"That's it?" Rivka wondered, but he was already gone. She closed and locked the door. Floyd joined Wenceslaus on the bed.

She crawled in quickly to claim her space. She found the two snoring animals comforting. "You've been in bed for five seconds, and you're already asleep? Oh, to be you."

Hope and despair. The inmates' competing emotions fought for primacy. She pushed those thoughts into the deep recesses of her mind and found enough peace to join Floyd and Wenceslaus in a deep sleep.

Planetary Hive, Bacaville, Planet Colay in the Barrier Nebula

Sahved walked at Chaz's side. The blocky building had tall and wide doorways to accommodate the Colay since they walked on all their legs close to the ground as readily as upright on two in humanoid fashion.

Lindy followed the two inside, where they didn't have to look for the location of the head offices. Chaz had already downloaded the plans and knew that the more important the person, the farther underground they worked.

Very much like the bugs they'd evolved from.

There was no elevator, just a wide-open circular passage sloping up and down, half stairs and half a smooth ramp. Although human feet would slip on it, the Colay's feet would hold steady. There was a center column that also served a purpose for those in a hurry going up or down. A Colay raced past them on the column. Sahved leaned over the opening and touched the surface.

"Feels like smooth marble."

"A death sentence if we tried to cling to it," Lindy offered.

Chaz continued downward without speculation or commentary. He'd been in charge of a group before, but this time, it felt different. He had the lead where Rivka normally would have been. He wasn't a diplomatic sort. He was still trying to sort out the nuances of coercion. Rivka exerted pressure when she had to, but most often, she was sufficiently convincing in her arguments to sway all but the perpetrators.

They had every reason to lie, but Rivka's gift saw through their duplicity.

He had no such subroutine.

I'll need you to tell me if you think they're lying, Chaz said privately to Sahved.

I will do my best, but I don't think this group is invested with Rising Sun. If not, then there should be no reason to prevaricate. We only need to speak to them about the danger of a monopoly.

Chaz agreed. That put his thoughts at ease and allowed him to focus on what he needed to do.

They followed a winding corridor through the bottom floor of the complex. Chaz made no missteps since he knew exactly where he was going.

They arrived ten minutes early for their appointment. There was nowhere to sit, but the floor was covered by a soft carpet. The Colay would have rested easily in its tender embrace. Chaz, Sahved, and Lindy stood. The receptionist didn't bother offering them refreshments.

Sahved was happy that he didn't have to put on a show by eating anything a race of cockroaches would think of as a delicacy.

When the time came, the queen stepped out on all of her legs. The trappings of office rested on her back. Chaz took a knee and bowed. Sahved and Lindy followed suit, but Lindy made sure she was pressed against the door to keep anyone from coming in behind them.

Clicks and shrieks preceded the translation chip's interpretation of the Colay language. "Welcome to Colay. Please." The queen reentered her office, which the team considered austere. A single desk with open slots instead of drawers had a padded plank raised to and over it for the queen to lie on while she worked. The computers didn't have two-dimensional screens. They showed a texture that could be more easily interpreted by multi-faceted eyes.

Chaz was fascinated by the technology, but now was not the time to explore it, and the queen was probably the wrong one to ask.

"We're here to discuss Rising Sun Industries and their practices that would violate antitrust laws in most other parts of the Federation," Chaz started. "It appears that Rising Sun Industries is following a template they've successfully used elsewhere to take over Colay assets. They are going to make life difficult for your people."

"The mining and production sector. We have little interest in managing those processes ourselves. We see their engagement as an outside investment in Colay's success. You're not xenophobic, are you?"

Sahved looked behind him. "I don't think so. We're all aliens here."

Clicks preceded the translation of the calm words spoken by the queen. "We appreciate what they are doing for us. We are already seeing improved prosperity. We will not give more to them unwittingly. Is that all?"

"It is. Thank you. We will stay in touch." A scent filled the room, odd and earthy.

"We are unable to replicate scents, but we can appreciate your kindness."

The queen bowed her head, and the trio once again took a knee before her. They left on their own as the queen returned to work.

Sahved nodded at the receptionist on the way out.

"I'm not sure the Magistrate will be happy with our progress," Sahved remarked.

"She committed to providing oversight. I'll have to review their laws to see what they might implement to reclaim ownership. And what does the appeals process look like?" Chaz replied. "It depends on how aggressive Rising Sun is in dominating the marketplace."

"But monopolies aren't illegal here," Sahved countered.

Chaz continued walking, but his gait was mechanical as

if he'd set his system's autopilot so he could continue his analysis. While they climbed the steps, he spoke. "I have to go back to the Magistrate's very first statement regarding this case. Why are we here?"

"To see if a crime has been committed," Sahved offered.

"When does that happen? The crime has always been committed by the time the Magistrate gets involved. Why here?"

"Malpace Frenzik is charismatic but distinctly unlikeable. He comes across as one who will not stop until he is in charge of everything."

Chaz continued his automaton routine across the first floor and out the door. "I had not come to that conclusion, but I can see that it makes sense. Illegal or not, it should be, and that is the premise under which we act. I suggest it is a slippery slope. We are not the ones to make the law."

"I know, Chaz. I am uncomfortable too, but not the most uncomfortable I've ever been. That was in the prison. That was most unpleasant, and I am convinced that Rising Sun Industries exacerbated the situation. I think we need to continue that line of inquiry."

"Do we let the planets fail before they come begging for help?" Chaz suggested.

Sahved didn't have an answer. They continued walking to a nearby park, where the invisible *Wyatt Earp* waited.

CHAPTER TWELVE

Wyatt Earp, in Orbit, Planet Colay in the Barrier Nebula

"What's next?" Red asked while eating an emergency ration bar. The others sat around the conference table.

"We wait," Chaz said. "The Magistrate is sleeping. We'll ask her after she awakens."

"Don't make me fight you," Tyler said from the corridor. "She's not returning to work until I clear her, so you might as well proceed with the investigation on the assumption that she's not available."

"Incoming call from Grainger. I'll reroute it here," Clevarious offered.

"Go ahead," Chaz said.

Dennicron leaned in. She was up to speed. The Singularity had improved their processes for reestablishing an SI's integration with a SCAMP body. The bad news was that they'd learned through practice because Chaz and Dennicron had had problems not foreseen in the original design.

They were the extreme. Chrysanthemum, the chief of

Federation Station 11, was more of what the designers had intended for daily engagement.

Grainger's face appeared three-dimensionally in the holographic display above the conference table.

"Where's Rivka?" he asked.

"She is currently on mandated bed rest. Doctor's orders," Tyler replied.

"Looking after the mental health of the team is important for long-term success," Grainger agreed. "Prognosis?"

"She'll be fine after she gets enough rest."

"We're managing this investigation in the meantime, although we are having a hard time finding a case," Chaz admitted. "On the face of it, prima facie, there is no case or controversy."

Sahved snapped his eyeballs to the SI. It wasn't what *he* would have told Grainger.

"Keep digging. I feel there's something there."

"Is our time and Rivka's health worth sacrificing on a fishing expedition?"

"Now you sound like a lawyer!" Grainger cheered. "Welcome to the team. Federation planets need to maintain their individual right to rule their people. This incursion by Rising Sun Industries threatens to upset the world-leadership dynamic that makes the Federation stronger. We would normally send an ambassador, and we will in time. You are putting them on notice, even if you don't find anything. For this issue, you are ambassadors for the Federation. I guess I could have made that clearer."

Sahved threw his hands up and shook his head.

"You have an issue with that, Sahved?"

"I'm sorry, Mr. Grainger. I did not mean to make my

confusion on our purpose so clear. Please excuse my outburst." Sahved bowed his head to Grainger's image.

"Since I have you guys all pissed off, the investigator from our office will arrive at Lewbamar later today. A four-legged Yollin lawyer. He's tenacious and will get to the truth."

"*FUCK THAT GUY!*" Red bellowed.

"Who said that?" Grainger's image looked around, but Red was in the corridor.

"I did." Red stepped into the room. "Tenacious. This motherfucker is going to come here to tear Rivka down and second-guess everything she did from the safety of his pansy-ass office. Tenacious! That's a word internal affairs types use for someone with a vendetta."

"Calm down." Grainger's fingers twitched as if he wanted to throttle someone. Red was already giving him the finger. He hated it when people told him to calm down. "All I meant was that he'll get to the truth."

"I'm gonna fight him," Red declared.

"You are *not* going to fight him." Grainger pointed a finger at him. "Hey, I hired you!"

Red huffed and crossed his arms. "I'm going to fight him."

"Chaz, Dennicron, Sahved, and all the rest of you. Please cooperate with the investigation. Kag'Mar is protecting the sanctity of this office. We are under the ambassadors' microscopes and have to be aboveboard at all times. They are watching us."

"*Bullshit!*" Red shouted. "They are watching Rivka. Those fuckers from Delegor and Foromme will continue to stir up shit. We should go back there and root them all out."

"They were very popular with their people, but that's beside the point."

"If you sacrifice Rivka on the altar of expediency, I'll fight you, too." Red glared at Grainger's image.

"We will not sacrifice Rivka. Convince Kag'Mar, and he'll be your undying champion. Any questions?"

"Does he have an itinerary yet?" Chaz asked.

"First visit will be to the prison. Establish a baseline and work backward from that."

"We'll be ready for his visit," Chaz confirmed.

"We have to do this," Grainger pressed. "And I don't want anyone to fight with Kag'Mar. He's not your enemy. He's an advocate just like Rivka."

"That's some major league lawyer bullshit," Red grumbled but not loud enough for Grainger to hear.

Grainger continued. "I know that you are all fanatically loyal to Rivka. Tell the truth. The best thing you can do to protect her is to advise her wisely and be the friends that you've grown to be. Keep everyone doing the right thing."

"Family," Red announced loudly. "We're family. My son? He's flying around here somewhere, and one of his aunts or uncles is watching over him. Same with Alanna. Same with Ankh...I mean Ambassador Ankh and Ambassador Erasmus. You want a neutral party, maybe ask Ankh to investigate. He's also an ambassador."

All eyes turned to Grainger.

"That's an interesting proposition. Neutral? Although he runs the embassy on Rivka's ship, I think his neutrality might be called to question in regard to All Guns Blazing and frequent deliveries to *Wyatt Earp* of significant quantities of food."

Chaz and Dennicron maintained their even expressions. The others looked away.

Red snapped his fingers. "The little guy loves AGB, and he'd feel guilty eating it without us."

"You and I both know Ankh would never feel guilty," Grainger replied. "No. It'll be Kag'Mar. Be cool, and Red, please don't fight him."

"I'll take it under advisement," the big bodyguard growled.

Grainger cut the signal without another word.

"I won't let him hurt Rivka," Red snarled.

"None of us will," Tyler confirmed. Chaz and Dennicron stared. Tyler stared back. "That means *none* of us."

"We will protect the sanctity of this office and this investigation. We were there. Rivka did nothing wrong."

"Then we won't have any problems with Kag'Mar." Red wasn't convinced. He'd never fought a four-legged Yollin before but was sure he could take him. He had no doubt he'd have to fight him. It was the Yollin way. It was also Red's way.

He had sworn to protect Rivka at all costs.

Chaz spoke aloud for everyone's benefit. "Set course for Lewbamar, best possible speed. Cloak and head directly to the prison. We will wait there."

"Now you're talking, Chaz." Red gave him two thumbs-up. He looked down the corridor. Rivka's door was still closed. She was out of action, and that was when she needed him the most.

. . .

Wyatt Earp, Hovering above the Crystal City Holding Cells, Planet Lewbamar in the Barrier Nebula

The crew filled the bridge and watched the screen, waiting for the investigator's arrival.

"Can we go with him?" Red asked.

"I will offer to accompany him," Chaz stated.

"We all want to go," Red responded. The others nodded vigorously.

"Not you," Chaz replied. "You made your feelings abundantly clear. We can't give the impression of trying to influence the investigation, not through disinformation or intimidation."

"Impression of trying to influence…" Red repeated. "We can influence it as long as we don't look like we're doing that. Check."

"Because we won't be doing it. You heard Grainger. We have to protect the sanctity of the office."

"Not if it jeopardizes Rivka in any way. Where would you be without her? I'll start. I'd be dead. There was a price on my head, and only one person took that seriously and did something about it. Lindy would be waiting tables. Clodagh would be the chief engineer on _War Axe_, but their policies regarding fraternization aren't as liberal as Rivka's. The only reason she and Cole are together is that Rivka brought them here. Sahved. Third deputy undersecretary to a pack of morons who had no respect for you. You'd still be there. Dead end.

"Sentient Intelligence. None of you would have any rights if it weren't for Rivka. Groenwyn? You'd be in jail for what you did on your home station and the issue with the spa. You would not be free. Lauton, wherever she is, head of a planet that specialized in money laundering. Not her fault, but others wouldn't have seen it that way. Rivka protected your innocence. Our pilots. Where would you be? I don't even know, but not here, not gallivanting around the universe, a boyfriend in every port."

At their look, he held up his hands.

"Just making a point," he continued. "All of us. Alanna, Dery, and the Rorke's Drift children who were born on *Wyatt Earp*, and if it hadn't been for Rivka, we wouldn't have a heavy frigate to call home. This ship is way bigger than she rates, but it's for all of us. The truth is, you're here because Rivka saw something in all of you and protected you even when you hadn't earned it. Just like me. You're the only family I have. Don't fuck that up. Anyone causes her problems, you'll deal with me."

Red wasn't one to stand on a soapbox and spill his guts, but this was his time to pay part of a bill that could never be paid.

He worked his way through the crowd without making eye contact. He felt like crying but would never let the others see him.

Dery flew into his face, and he reacted by bending backward. The boy landed on his chest, almost toppling Red.

He straightened with great effort, holding the boy in his arm. "Hi, big man. Who are you helping today?"

Dad, the boy replied.

"Me? I'm solid as a continent. Maybe talk to Rivka? We could really use her." Red looked deeply into the boy's eyes.

Peace.

"Peace through superior firepower," Red replied.

Peace.

"He's coming to give Rivka a hard time. I can't have that, little man."

The boy returned his look.

"Oh, jeez," Red blurted. "It's like getting kicked in the 'nads."

Peace.

"Can't you get him to think peaceful thoughts? *Tenacious.* He's coming here to prove himself. If he were a neutral party looking to find the truth, then I wouldn't be so hard on him."

Dery kept his gaze focused on his father.

"Fine, little man. Unless he gives me no choice."

No.

Red hugged his son and rushed for his quarters. He didn't want the others to see him. He felt helpless and torn. He pushed through the door and slammed it behind him. He hugged Dery close but fought the tears. He wouldn't let go. He couldn't.

The fight was coming, and he was ill-equipped for this one.

"He's here," Clodagh announced.

"Take us down," Chaz ordered. "Sahved and I will meet Kag'Mar."

Red didn't glare at them. He was trying to listen to his son. He didn't want to fail the boy, but he couldn't fail Rivka, either.

"I should go, too," Groenwyn offered in a small voice.

"No need. This isn't about who was there but about those who are investigators. We will be able to provide insight, and although Dennicron and I recorded everything from that day, Dennicron's recording was destroyed with the short. She has no memory of what happened at the prison."

"Thank you." Groenwyn looked pale. Lauton was keeping her upright.

"When will you need my analysis of the finances?" Lauton asked.

"As soon as it's ready. Give it to Dennicron if we're not back."

"It's not ready. I have a way to go."

Chaz made his perplexed face. "Then what are you doing out here?"

The red-skinned woman pointed at Groenwyn. Chaz motioned toward their quarters. "Rivka isn't the only one who needs to heal." Lauton stuck her tongue out at Chaz but conceded and guided Groenwyn toward their cabin.

"Right!" Chaz declared. He headed for the airlock as *Wyatt Earp* descended. Still cloaked, the ship drew no unwanted attention. A shuttle approached the small landing pad a short distance from the front entrance.

Wyatt Earp settled on the other side. Chaz punched the button and the side hatch opened, then the ramp deployed to touch the soft grass growing outside of the prison.

Only outside. Nothing grew within its confines.

The shuttle landed and opened its door. A single figure walked out. Four legs, a centaur but not. The Yollin had a carapace on its upper body, with mandibles on both sides of a wide mouth. Kag'Mar walked with confidence.

Chaz and Sahved intercepted him before he reached the front door.

"Can I assume you are Chaz and Sahved? None of the others are here?" He hadn't seen them depart *Wyatt Earp*.

"Just us. We were the investigators on scene. We'll answer your questions based on what you see at this facility," Chaz replied smoothly.

Better, Sahved sent. *The truth is a relative beast based on the question asked.*

You sound like Rivka, but she is wise. It's okay to sound like her.

"My name is Kag'Mar. I'm here on behalf of the High Chancellor's office to investigate the incident being referred to as 'the Crystal City Holding Cells Massacre.'"

Chaz and Sahved remained between Kag'Mar and the entrance. He looked past them and then back at them, implying that they were holding him up.

"There's power in names. There's power in attachments. Calling it a massacre and saying that you are investigating Magistrate Rivka Anoa in accordance with it presupposes a guilt that the Magistrate should not be besmirched with. Innocent until proven guilty. Have you already made your decision?" Chaz pressed.

"Of course not. I have a lot of questions to be answered first. But your point is valid. We need no unnecessary implications. We shall call it the..." He hesitated. "What would you recommend?"

Chaz smiled. "Thank you for asking. Just call it the investigation into the Crystal City Holding Cells. Simpler is better. The only incontrovertible fact so far is that this is the Crystal City Holding Cells."

"And you were both there. That is a fact as well, by your own admission."

"We acknowledge that your investigation has already started. Shall we?" Chaz stepped aside and gestured at the door. The Yollin passed the two. Chaz and Sahved fell in behind him.

Once inside, they walked up to the desk officer, where Kag'Mar introduced himself.

Sahved nudged Chaz and pointed at the door leading to the interior of the cell block. It stood open and unguarded.

The Yollin waited for the administrator to acknowledge him.

When he finally looked up, he flinched at the sight of mandibles, but then his eyes found Chaz and Sahved. "You!" He pointed at them while his mouth worked wordlessly.

"I'd like to review the events from two days past as part of Federation oversight. This means interviews," Kag'Mar explained, "and review of any physical materials you might have related to the *riot*."

Sahved nodded approvingly.

"Go on in. The staff has nothing to do since all the prisoners died." He stabbed a thumb over his shoulder and returned to his terminal.

Sahved cautiously took a step toward the doorway, but Kag'Mar wasn't finished with the desk officer. "What do you mean they're all dead?"

"They're dead. They fought the guards and got themselves killed," he explained impatiently. "Anything else?"

"Security footage from your video surveillance, please."

"We don't have any of that. No cameras back there." He gestured with his head toward the pens.

"I'll be back," Kag'Mar warned. He pointed for Chaz and Sahved to go inside. Once there, he stopped them. "On the Magistrate's report, she most specifically stated that a number of the prisoners surrendered to the guards. Video footage taken by *Wyatt Earp* supported those statements."

"I have my video recordings, too, from my perspective on the ground. Unfortunately, we lost Dennicron's when she shorted upon impact with the electric fence."

"You have video?"

"Of course. I am a sentient intelligence residing within a self-contained artificial mobility platform, a SCAMP. I am a citizen of the Singularity."

"I see. Apparently, I wasn't told everything so my opinion wouldn't be unduly influenced. I'll need that recording as soon as you can send it. If I might ask, why wasn't it included in the original report?"

"I was unavailable. Dennicron is my partner, and she was injured. One hundred percent of my focus was on assessing the damage and making the repairs. That took nearly eighteen hours. We are lucky to be co-located with Ambassadors Ankh and Erasmus. Their assistance was critical in bringing Dennicron back online so quickly."

"I look forward to meeting her." Kag'Mar studied Chaz's features far more closely than he had earlier.

"The video has been forwarded," Chaz confirmed.

"Extraordinary. I would love to have an SI in our office. You would make us better."

Chaz beamed. They continued to a catwalk from which they could look down on the pens. Not a single Lewbamarian remained. The door to the stairway stood open. They descended the stairs.

Kag'Mar turned left and walked toward the pens. Chaz and Sahved had not gone that way previously. The last time they were there, they had been led outside.

Sahved coughed at the smell. Even the Yollin was not immune to it. He took a couple steps into the pen before signaling that he'd seen enough.

"All of their prisoners were in this one space?"

"All of them. They ate, slept, and relieved themselves right there," Chaz replied.

"How many would you say were here?"

Chaz didn't have to guess. His systems had counted them. "The exact number was five hundred and fifteen."

"In that one space? That's not quite up to Federation standard. Even Jhiordaan treats prisoners a hundred times better than that."

Sahved held his tongue. Despite their appearance, the Lewbamarians had a barbaric streak that was nearly unrivaled.

They proceeded down the corridor and outside and found that the fence had not been repaired following the break. The ground was stained with Lewbamarian blood.

CHAPTER THIRTEEN

The Yard, Crystal City Holding Cells, Planet Lewbamar in the Barrier Nebula

"Can you explain where you were and what happened, please? I've read the report, but I'd like to visualize it as seen through your eyes," Kag'Mar requested.

Sahved moved to where he had stood. Chaz took his position and pointed out exactly where each member of the team had been, emphasizing that the focus had been on Rivka and her ability to see into the prisoners' minds.

"And she has to touch them to gain that insight. I understand." Kag'Mar looked closely at the ground while Chaz and Sahved waited.

"It happened rather quickly. They turned all the prisoners loose at once. The inmates ran down that corridor," Chaz pointed, "and into the yard as fast as they could go. They turned on us the instant we tried to slow them down so the Magistrate could process what she saw in their minds. They were passing too quickly."

"How did she do it?" Kag'Mar leaned close.

Chaz demonstrated. "She touched them on their shoulders as they passed. She kept shouting the same question. "Who was paid to commit crimes?"

"That's all she needs to do?"

"It brings the memory, and if I understand correctly, the emotions to the surface where she can most easily see them. You'll have to ask her since anything you get from me about it would be hearsay."

The Yollin raised his hand. He wasn't going to press the issue.

"And once the Lewbamarians attacked you, you made a run for it."

"Returning the way we'd come wasn't going to work. The corridor was filled with prisoners. There was no swimming against that tide." Chaz was proud of his usage of idiomatic expressions.

"The guards provided no support? No oversight?"

"They showed us out here and returned up the staircase, locking us in."

"What was this line of inquiry that led Rivka here? In her report, she stated that after the arrests, the criminals were complaining about not getting paid."

"Exactly that. We heard it from the potentate, and yes, he has every reason to lie, but the Magistrate saw things in the minds of some prisoners that confirmed it. But the one who paid them was a Lewbamarian. They weren't directly paid by Rising Sun, only through an intermediary if that link holds up to scrutiny. We're examining financial records for Crystal City as well as the records for Rising Sun Industries."

The Yollin nodded. "After you were attacked by the prisoners, what did you do?"

Chaz ran toward the fence and vaulted through. "I did that to breach the fence to allow our people to get out. The Lewbamarians tried to follow, but in their haste, they weren't as cognizant of the electrified fence."

"Is it still active?"

Chaz gripped it. "No. It is powered down."

The Yollin squeezed through the gap, but despite the calm of the moment and being deliberate, he touched the fence on both sides. "Your people ran through here with an angry mob following?"

"No," Sahved interjected. "The mob wasn't angry; they sought freedom. Conditions were so harsh in here that they were willing to die for this one chance to escape. They didn't care about us. They only wanted to reach the other side of the fence."

"Where the green grass grows despite the chill," Kag'Mar intoned as if reading poetry.

They led him around the perimeter to where they had to pull Dennicron free.

Kag'Mar had to grab the fence and stretch it aside to get back into the enclosed compound known as the yard. He shivered, but not from the cold Lewbamarian air.

They returned inside and to the second floor, where they found the guard break room half-filled. They could find no other guards.

Kag'Mar held his credentials before him. "Kag'Mar from the Federation." He stretched and clicked his mandibles. Sometimes witnesses needed a show of force to tell what they knew. "Who was working two days ago during the prisoner escape?"

They all raised their hands.

"Why did you kill all the prisoners?" he asked abruptly.

"They were trying to escape," a gruff voice replied. The owner stood. His fur was shot through with gray, and a scar ran over the top of his head.

"The escape attempt was stalled by the ship. I have images showing the prisoners prostrate in the yard."

He flicked a hand. "After the ship left, they tried to escape."

"The bloodstains I just observed were centered in the yard, exactly where the prisoners were when *Wyatt Earp* departed with the Magistrate and her crew. Help me understand how this could be."

"Don't know. It was ugly. They were escaping. That's punishable by death," the guard said. "It's not my problem."

"Who ordered the guards to shoot the prisoners?"

"Ordered? It's a standing order. The general alarm sounded, which means there's a prison break in progress. We don't tolerate that. The penalty is death."

"Even if they weren't breaking out," Kag'Mar pressed.

"They were all breaking out."

Sahved stood with his mouth open and his head cocked to one side. "Who sounded the alarm since it was ringing before we broke through the fence?"

The guards shrugged. "Not us."

On the wall was a switch labeled Alarm. "What's that?" Kag'Mar pointed.

"The alarm, but none of us switched it on," the guard claimed.

"Where else can the alarm be turned on?"

"Desk Officer. Warden. That's about it."

"Both locations are outside the pens."

"The warden can see the yard from his office. Next level up."

"Thank you for your cooperation," Kag'Mar said. The guards had cooperated without motivation and been slightly hostile, but they had answered his questions.

The Yollin quickly walked off the catwalk and went back to the area outside the cell area.

He stopped by the desk officer. "Which way to the warden's office, please?"

"He's not here."

The group waited for more information, but nothing was forthcoming.

Kag'Mar took control. "Where can we find him? We are at a critical stage of our investigation, and I need to talk with him right now."

"He's not here. What else can I say?"

"You can tell me where he is; that's what you can say. We will go to him. Tell me."

"Government compound. Meeting with Mr. Ahsooleyman."

"Unsurprisingly," Chaz commented. "We can take *Wyatt Earp*."

Kag'Mar followed Chaz and Sahved out of the building. The side hatch appeared out of thin air, and the ramp descended.

"Your ship is invisible?" Kag'Mar stated.

"Barrister," Sahved started, "stating the obvious?"

"Isn't that what lawyers are good at?"

"I'm still learning, but it seems so." Sahved smiled at the Yollin.

Red waited inside the airlock. He was dressed for combat.

Chaz moved in front of Kag'Mar. "Stand down, Red. He's on our side."

"How'd you come to that conclusion?" Red growled.

"The second we saw that they had killed all the prisoners. There are no inmates left."

Red's posture changed, and his face fell. "I don't exactly like the Lewbamarians, but I'm pretty sure those poor souls didn't deserve to die. All of them? We left a shitload in the yard on their faces."

"Looked like they killed them all right where we last saw them," Sahved replied.

"That's the most fucked-up thing I've ever heard. Is that legal? Isn't that genocide or something?" Red suggested.

"It's not, actually." Chaz continued into the airlock. "Under the Lewbamarian legal system, once incarcerated, the individuals are subject to the sentence terms, which can be carried out at the state's discretion."

"And all sentences are terminal," Kag'Mar added while Red cleared the airlock by entering the ship.

"Every crime is a capital crime," Chaz confirmed. "It might be the most extreme legal system in the Federation. Surprising that they'd have a crime wave *after* this penalty was in effect. It is understandable that such an extreme sentence would be implemented in response to a crime wave but not before. The pendulum swing, as flesh and blood actions and reactions could be described."

Once Sahved was inside, he punched the button and secured the hatch.

"Nice ship," Kag'Mar stated. He didn't hold out his hand to Red, who blocked the corridor to the bridge. The two faced off.

Chaz tried to get Red's attention. "I said, he's on our side."

"I'm Rivka's bodyguard."

"Isn't that pleasant?" Kag'Mar replied, easing closer to the human until they were nearly carapace to chest.

"No fighting!" Chaz bellowed.

Dery came upon the group from behind, flew past them, and landed on Kag'Mar's back. Red's features softened.

"Hey, what's going on back there?" Kag'Mar twisted around to see the part-faerie looking at him. "What are you?"

Der'ayd'nil, the boy replied. *Peace.*

"Yes, of course. I'm Kag'Mar, a Yollin. We tend not to shy away from weak attempts at physical intimidation."

"That's my son, jagoff," Red growled.

"Yes, I noticed the resemblance," Kag'Mar replied smoothly. He faced Red.

Then he offered his hand.

Red took it, and the test of wills began. They gripped. Red grinned, although his lip sporadically twitched. The Yollin's mandibles clicked with his efforts.

"Smart boy." Kag'Mar grunted again.

"Good thing he doesn't take after me," Red replied, straining to make the words sound normal.

Dery fluttered between the two, then continued toward

the bridge. Red and Kag'Mar held each other's eyes, bodies straining with their efforts.

"Shall we?" Kag'Mar offered.

"You first."

"After you. I insist."

Lindy came up behind them and shouted, "Don't make me shove a bistok prod up your horses' asses!"

The Yollin snorted. "The mother, I presume?"

Red started to laugh and let go of the Yollin's hand. "You presume correctly." He gestured with his head while rubbing the feeling back into his hand, and the group started moving. Red turned tour guide for his new friend, describing the ship and its spaces as they passed.

They stopped at the conference room. The Yollin squeezed in and stood off to the side. "My first complaint," he intoned. "A non-Yollin friendly ship. You need to upgrade."

"We *rescued* the ship from Skaine raiders," Red quipped. "It has been upgraded rather significantly with the improvement to the smell alone."

"Skaines? You guys get around, don't you?"

"Then there was the time we went to a little planet called Benitus Seven. Ever hear of the Skrima? No, it's because our man Ankh helped prevent a rift from getting blown open or something like that. There were some technical details I couldn't quite follow. Well, all of the technical details."

"I have neither heard of Benitus Seven nor the Screamers, but I don't usually leave Yoll. That's where my business is." He looked at Red. "I have no agenda except to make sure the office of the High Chancellor is beyond reproach.

That means the Magistrates have to be beyond reproach. From what I've seen, Magistrate Anoa was set up either to be killed in a horrible accident or kill all the witnesses. In either case, there's a vein of darkness that runs deep under the skin of Crystal City."

"Skrima," Chaz corrected. "But your eloquence is masterful."

Kag'Mar looked around the room. "I still need to conduct my investigation, which means I need to interview all of you privately, one by one, and I ask that you not talk with each other in between."

"Aren't we on our way to intercept the warden and talk to him?"

Kag'Mar blinked rapidly. "Yes. Let's do that first."

Red frowned. He wasn't as confident in the Yollin lawyer's abilities as he had been a minute earlier. "Gear up, people. Let's go see the Asshole Man and his lackey." Red walked off without waiting for a reply.

He ran into Dery in the corridor.

"I'm sorry, little man."

Rivka, Dery replied. *She is ready.*

Red turned around and ran into Sahved. "Gangway, coming through!" He hurried past the group and around the Yollin to get to Rivka's quarters. He tapped a knuckle gently on the door.

Rivka opened it instantly. She was dressed and in her Magistrate's jacket. Floyd came bouncing out and raced down the corridor like a bowling ball heading for the pins. They both watched as she hit Lauton and Groenwyn from behind, taking them down. They bounced off the Yollin's rump on their way to the deck.

Kag'Mar staggered and grabbed Dennicron for support. She held firm and stopped the cascade failure in its tracks.

Red turned his attention back to the Magistrate. "Are you okay?"

"Dery said I should go with you. I rested more than usual. We should probably go before Tyler sees me…"

"Too late," the ship's doctor replied. "I haven't released you yet."

"But you will, and there's no time like the present." She smiled warmly. After a quick kiss, she left him behind to walk down the corridor side-by-side with Red.

"It's not supposed to work that way," Tyler called after her. He shook his head and gave up. This wasn't an issue he wanted to fight her on, and she looked remarkably better. "Fine!"

Red pointed at the Yollin helping Groenwyn and Lauton up while Floyd raced back and forth under his belly. "Our investigator, Kag'Mar. Not a total jag. He sees the Lewbamarian failures. I don't think he's found anything that might fault you or the team."

Rivka nodded, observing Kag'Mar.

"We're off to find the warden. He's supposedly with the Albions."

"By 'with,' you mean he's working for them? When did that happen?"

"By with, I mean he's physically at Asshole Man's office, reporting on something or other. Oh! You missed the biggest news. The prison is empty. They killed all the prisoners. Every last one of them."

"Even those who escaped into the woods?"

Red stopped. "No one said anything about them, and none of us asked."

"We can ask the warden," Rivka offered, slapping Red on the back. They reached the group. "Kag'Mar, I'm Rivka Anoa. Pleased to meet you." She worked her way to where they could shake hands, but he declined.

"Nothing personal. Let's keep our thoughts to ourselves, shall we?"

Rivka shrugged one shoulder. "I'll tell you anything you want to know. We have no secrets here. Grainger told us to cooperate, so that's what we'll do. How do you find the crew so far?"

"They are congenial and fanatically loyal, almost cult-like."

"Now, now. You don't need to use emotionally charged words with me. They are indeed as loyal to me as I am to them. It's the synergy that keeps us moving in lockstep, a well-oiled machine, as it may be, although with frictionless bearings. I guess that's not really a saying anyone modern uses."

"Will there be All Guns Blazing later? I've heard stories about how you're able to get deliveries."

Wyatt Earp touched down. "We are inside the governmental compound," Clevarious broadcast through the ship.

"All ashore who's going ashore. I'll be joining you," Rivka stated.

"I'm not sure that's a good idea," Kag'Mar replied.

"It's still my investigation. You are investigating me unless you've been reassigned as the lead on this case. Have you?"

"I have not." Kag'Mar clicked his mandibles and stared.

"Then you watch me. I'll handle the questions."

"Are you planning to use your special technique?"

"Planning? Interesting turn of phrase. We shall see, won't we?" Rivka almost patted his back but stopped before touching him. "Red, Lindy, Sahved, and Chaz, with me."

"And me?" Dennicron asked.

"Was your memory of the prison restored? Oh, and glad to see you're up and about."

Dennicron smiled. "I am back but have no memory from when I left the ship until I woke up in the embassy."

The Embassy of the Singularity, also known as *Wyatt Earp's* engineering section.

"Then you stay behind. We already have a lot of people."

"I remember it all," Groenwyn told her.

"And it wasn't our fault. I'm going to lean on the warden to see what he knows. You don't need to come. Stay here and keep working with Lauton on the finances, even if your only role is to get her fizzy drinks and snacks. Maybe talk with Ankh about an AGB delivery?"

Groenwyn forced a smile. "Will do. Thanks, Magistrate." She and Lauton ambled away.

Red made a face and shook his head. They'd shown up at the meeting of their own accord. No one had invited them.

Loyalty, Rivka thought. All hands on deck to defend her honor. Kag'Mar would have his hands full interviewing them, and Rivka had no problem with that. Cult. There was no penalty for leaving. There was an indoctrination. There was a shared belief in Justice. They worked for each other. They worked for the Federation.

Kag'Mar would see that. Probably already had. He was attempting to get under their skin to see if they would break under pressure.

There was nothing to break.

Rivka wanted to touch Kag'Mar and get into his mind, but she didn't dare. She had to trust that Grainger wouldn't send an investigator with an agenda.

Still, his presence and demeanor made her angry.

She'd have to get over it. She had an investigation to conduct. Would Rising Sun Industries survive her inquiries and judgment or not?

The jury was still out.

CHAPTER FOURTEEN

<u>Crystal City Governmental Compound, Planet Lewbamar</u>

Red led the way to the potentate's office, now occupied by Ahsooleyman in his role of overseer of Crystal City.

They passed an old, pudgy Lewbamarian on the way. Red thought he looked familiar and waved to get Chaz's attention. He recognized him from a picture on the wall of the holding cells.

"Warden," Chaz greeted the Lewbamarian.

The elderly male tried to hurry his steps, but Lindy blocked him. Rivka eased up to him and waved her credentials in his face. "Magistrate Rivka Anoa, but you already knew that, didn't you?"

He shrugged and backed up until he ran into the wall. Rivka moved close. He glanced at her hands.

"You've been briefed. Since you are a member of the law enforcement community, you'll appreciate that I'm obligated to use all the tools at my command to get to the truth. Who ordered you not to cooperate with my investigation?"

Her hand shot out to grab his collar and keep him pinned against the wall.

An Albion. Belloward.

"Many of the new prisoners were paid to commit crimes, weren't they? You were responsible for making sure they didn't talk."

He winced, knowing his thoughts had betrayed him.

Heavy footfalls pounded down the corridor toward them. Rivka didn't bother to look. She had people who would hold them back. She trusted her people with her life.

The warden had been paid to silence the prisoners, and worse, he'd been paid to facilitate the crimes they'd committed. Who better to know the city's less than reputable souls, even if they were never in his prison? He'd known them by their reputation with the prisoners, and for a few extra morsels in their dinner bowls, they'd told him who and where.

Rivka let go. The warden refused to meet her eyes.

"What's going on here? I demand that you allow that individual to pass right now!" Ahsooleyman shouted, but Red held him off.

"Every crime on Lewbamar is punishable by death. The conspiracy you committed should be a death sentence by your own admission."

"I never said a word," he claimed weakly while continuing to stare at the floor.

"You and I both know that you don't have to. You took orders from Belloward to stop my investigation. And for everyone's edification, you also took credits to hire those criminals in the first place. You created the crime wave that put Rising Sun Industries in power. That means, contractually, that element is null and void. I'll be removing Rising Sun from its position of authority over Crystal City.

"And you. What do I do with you?"

Rivka wrapped her hand around the warden's throat.

Kag'Mar stepped in and seized her arm. She snapped at him, "What's your agenda?"

He staggered back, but it was too late.

He wanted to be a Magistrate and learn from the best.

"Your technique for learning sucks, but it is *very* Yollin to be aggressive and confrontational. There's no need for that." Rivka said. She turned back to the warden, having not let go of his throat. "I need a written statement with a full confession. That will mitigate the life sentence I've given you."

He finally looked up. Ahsooleyman was fuming.

"Red, throw him out."

The Albion was big but not a fighter. He crouched in a wrestler's stance. Red didn't hesitate. He delivered an uppercut to the chin that shot the alien upright. Ahsooleyman wobbled for a moment before toppling over.

"I thought you'd be tougher than that," Red told the unconscious body.

Rivka returned to the warden. "Who paid you to pay the Lewbamarians?"

"I don't know," he said, holding out his arm for Rivka to touch. "I never saw them, but it was an Albion."

"That doesn't sound very convincing." Rivka glanced toward the scraping of a body being dragged along the carpet. "Stop."

Red was heading toward a window to the outside. "You said to throw him out!"

She rolled her eyes and shook her head.

Red grumbled under his breath.

"I want to talk with him. Let's see who was manipulating the warden."

"That's it!" the warden proclaimed, seeking a lifeline to protect himself. "I was being manipulated."

"By your own greed. You took money, and I suspect you live a lavish lifestyle. Take the Mrs. on a grand vacation anywhere?"

His respite was short-lived. He sighed and returned to staring at the floor.

"I was misled," he mumbled.

"I believe you," Rivka replied. "Did they promise you that once they were in charge, you would be in the clear? You don't need to answer that now. Put it in your written statement."

Ahsooleyman stirred. Red looked for direction. He reared back and readied a fist.

"Stand him up. I'll talk with him."

Rivka nodded for Chaz to watch the warden. She sauntered up to Ahsooleyman. He was taller than Red and twice as wide as Rivka, but he had gone down with a single punch. "The bigger they are…"

Ahsooleyman rubbed his jaw. His eyes wouldn't open more than halfway.

Rivka waited for him to gather his wits.

"You've been a bad boy, Mr. Ahsooleyman."

His head lolled.

"How hard did you hit him?" Rivka asked.

"I thought he was tougher." Red shrugged and surveyed the area. Only Lewbamarians were watching. No other Albions were in the area. "What about Belloward?"

"We'll find him. Interplanetary crime. I doubt either this one or Frenzik will cover for him. They'll hang him out to dry." Rivka nudged Ahsooleyman. "You awake yet?"

He was well enough to glare at her.

"Who paid the warden?" Rivka held onto his arm. He tried to shrug away but couldn't. It had been him. "Did Frenzik know?"

Ahsooleyman had made sure Frenzik didn't know.

"But he had to!" Rivka snarled. "Ahsooleyman and Belloward are both going to Jhiordaan. Secure him and bring him with us. Chaz and Sahved, find Belloward."

The two nodded and hurried away.

Rivka took a shortcut and gripped his arm afresh. "Where's Belloward?"

The archives. Ahsooleyman pulled away before raising his hand in a balled fist and snarling. Red hit him with a piledriver blow to the side of his head. The Albion went down a second time.

Try the archives, she told Chaz. "Why are you just standing there and not writing down everything you know?"

"Glass jaw." Red chuckled. He rolled him over and sat him upright, even though he was still unconscious. Red kneeled and dipped to get his shoulder into Ahsooleyman's midsection, then pulled him onto his shoulder and grunted with the effort to stand. "Glass jaw but made of lead. This fucker is heavier than you, Magistrate."

"Very funny." She looked at the warden, who continued to cower against the wall. "Where's my written statement?"

He held up his hands to show his helplessness.

"Bring him," she ordered Kag'Mar. "We're going back to the ship."

The warden moaned.

"Would you stop?" She poked him in the chest with a finger. "Once your statement is done with sufficient detail that satisfies me, you'll be free to go, but I'll be keeping an eye on you. Mistreat another prisoner, and you'll be in Jhiordaan alongside these two." She pointed at Red, who was carrying Ahsooleyman. "Well, that one and Belloward."

They headed for the elevator.

"We better tell the potentate that he has his office back, and not to be such an idiot this time," Rivka muttered softly. Her team consisted of Red, who was carrying an Albion who made Red look tiny, Kag'Mar, who held the warden's arm, and Lindy, who was providing security for them all. Rivka had to dig deeper into the assets available to her. *Clevarious, please contact the potentate and have him meet me at my ship as soon as possible.*

The ship's still invisible, Magistrate, Clevarious replied.

De-invisible it, Rivka ordered quickly before correcting herself. *Turn off the cloak. They know we're here. And clear the corridors. We're bringing two Albion prisoners for immediate transfer to the next prison ship going to Jhiordaan.*

Clear the corridors. A new order Rivka had to give because that was where children and animals might be found now that *Wyatt Earp* had become a generational ship.

It took two elevators to get the team to the first floor.

Rivka strolled out as if she owned the place, unlike the last time, where she had left in confusion due to the conflicting and, as it turned out, fake information she had been given.

She was back in control and had the answers she needed to move forward.

The only missing piece was Malpace Frenzik. Organizations didn't become corrupt at lower levels if their leaders didn't encourage it. What did Frenzik know, and when had he learned it?

It was the age-old white-collar-crime question.

The ones who were impacted the worst by Ahsooleyman's and Belloward's crimes were those in prison who had been put to death. Criminal conspiracy resulting in hundreds of deaths. Not the usual white-collar crime. Proving the conspiracy had involved the chairman of Rising Sun Industries would require digging deep into the corporation's finances. They had everything as they related to Lewbamar but were missing the biggest piece of the corporate puzzle.

"We need to go to Albion," Rivka stated.

"That'll be fun," Red joked. He had to turn his whole body to answer and almost lost his balance when he swung Ahsooleyman around.

"I know you're being sarcastic. You don't want to go into Rising Sun's headquarters any more than I do, especially not if they are surging in wealth and power. Employees tend not to like government regulators who upset the apple cart."

"Good thing we're not regulators."

"They won't cooperate," Rivka posited. "We'll seize the data, and then we'll take a closer look. I think this is what

Grainger suspected—a growing monopoly led by a narcissist. I absolutely won't allow another Nefas to get a foothold in this galaxy."

They reached the ship after a brisk hike through the Crystal City chill. "Dump him in the brig and take that one to the conference room to prepare his statement. Clevarious, help him write it and then get a digital signature. I'll review it before we kick him off my ship."

Rivka continued to her quarters while Red dumped the Albion into the ship's padded brig and Kag'Mar escorted the warden to the conference room.

"Magistrate," the Yollin called while blocking the doorway to the conference room so the warden could work.

Rivka stopped and returned to him.

"I'm not part of your crew. I'm investigating an incident in which you took part."

"And your point?"

"I shouldn't be doing this. I need to conduct my investigation."

"Sure, no problem. Lindy, can you come to the conference room, please?" Rivka spoke in a normal tone of voice. Kag'Mar looked up and down the corridor. Red was fighting with the Albion, who had roused and didn't appreciate being locked up. A front kick sent him backward into the brig. Red secured the door and walked toward them.

Lindy came from the other direction. "I'll do it," Red said.

"I got it," Lindy replied.

"Figure it out. I don't care who watches this guy. Let me see his statement before he goes."

"Of course," Lindy said, raising her chin to her husband. Red surrendered. It wasn't a fight he cared to engage in.

"I'll catch a shower to get the Albion's stench off me." He winked and strolled past.

Lindy waved the Magistrate and Kag'Mar away.

"Anything else?" Rivka asked.

He shuffled his feet but didn't move. She waited.

"You looked into my mind unbidden." He raised his head to look at her.

"You grabbed me unbidden. You did that at your risk, knowing what I could do with that. Magistrates have zero time to pamper mass murderers, and that's exactly what that creature in there is."

"But you're going to let him go."

She smiled. "You know little of the ways of the wider galaxy. *I'm* letting him go, but I'm going to send a report on his activities to the potentate. I expect the warden will end up in that very same prison but on the wrong side of the bars. He will reap what he sowed. His crime was horrendous, but it wasn't a Federation crime unless they asked for help in resolving it, which they did not. The alien interference on this planet? That becomes immediately important to the Federation."

"We're aliens."

"Everyone who isn't from Lewbamar is an alien here. How much we're going to let them influence and subsequently take over for Lewbamarians is alien interference."

Kag'Mar slowly nodded his understanding.

"Anything else?" Rivka asked.

"What did you see within my mind?"

"Topical thoughts. The clearest is based on the immediate question. Most everything else is buried. Let me ask you, do you think you could do this job?"

"To be honest…" he started, and Rivka interrupted him.

"Why would you be anything but honest with me? It was a fair question."

"Just a saying. I have no intention of lying to you. I expect I would be quickly found out otherwise. In any case, I'm questioning my understanding of what it is you do. We have a glamorous view of a Magistrate swooping in and saving the day, not a daily fight with the locals and pushing the envelope of legality as a means to an end."

His eyes pleaded with Rivka to tell him he was wrong, but she couldn't do that.

"Welcome to the Magistrate channel. There is no source-book, no guidebook. We have the framework of the law, and we have the needs of the Federation. We balance those to do the best we can, but generally, we're making it up as we go to help the average Joe live his or her life as they see fit.

"A solid legal foundation lets them do that. People know what they can count on. Their credits are going to be in the system come morning. They are safe on the streets, and their home is safe when they are away. Isn't that as much as anyone could ask?"

"It's what civilized society is based on. Disparate peoples living together under an agreed-to set of guide-lines." Kag'Mar leaned against the wall while his mandibles clicked with his running thoughts. "I see."

"And judge-made law. That's us. Like the recognition and awarding of individual rights to the evolved intelligences out there now gathered as a collective under the

Singularity. High Chancellor Wyatt made that determination based on a case that I raised."

He nodded. Everyone was aware of that since it had created some turmoil, although those who were against the law were considered to be slaveowners. They quickly backed down, but the seething continued below the surface.

"I have a lot to think about. I don't know what questions I'll ask you as part of my investigation, but I know what I need to ask Sahved and Groenwyn."

"If you insist. I suggest the need for your investigation will be obviated by the statement of that individual in there." Rivka pointed at the conference room.

"Yes, but I want to make sure no one can question the report's findings. The Magistrate corps is under the microscope. Everything you do will be second-guessed for some time to come."

Rivka understood. She waved and walked away. She called over her shoulder before she reached her quarters, "For the record, don't touch me, and I won't touch you."

Kag'Mar watched her go. His report would be thorough, but she was right. She had been set up, and the warden's statement would clear her. He wanted to include in his report that in spite of the circumstances, her team had acted appropriately in pursuit of the truth and responded with the greatest restraint.

He'd get that report written before questioning the crew. He'd seen what he needed to see.

"Hey!" Red bellowed down the corridor. "Is this case over? Are we calling it? Bettors want to know."

Rivka poked her head into the corridor. "What the hell is wrong with you?"

"You're not involved in the betting, so someone has to make sure it's done right," Red replied. "Is the case closed?"

"Not by a long shot, Red. Not until we know whether Malpace Frenzik is involved. Is he going to Jhiordaan with his underlings or not? That's what inquiring minds want to know. Are they back with Belloward yet? I want to get out of here."

Lindy pointed at the conference room.

"By all that's holy, write faster!" Rivka shouted. Lindy looked into the room and chuckled at how easily the warden was flustered.

"Almost done," she answered for the one in her charge.

A commotion around the bend of the corridor signaled Chaz's and Sahved's arrival. An Albion voice roared in agony.

"Does no one want to cooperate?" Rivka asked rhetorically.

Lindy made space while Red headed to the brig. The Yollin excused himself and moved through the airlock to the cargo bay. Chaz held both of Belloward's arms behind his back. That led to most of the consternation since his arms had been dislocated from the shoulder sockets.

"Blowhard, you'll join Asshole Man," Red stated. He checked the monitor and spoke softly. "Move away from the door, or I'll zap you with enough energy to boil water."

The Albion delivered a series of hand gestures that Red didn't recognize but suspected were rude. Ahsooleyman backed away but readied himself.

"Stay back," Red called over his shoulder to Chaz. He

unlocked the door, and it opened. Ahsooleyman rushed through the opening. Red tripped him, and he went face-first into the opposite wall. With an effort, Red lifted him, spun him around, and tossed him headfirst back into the brig.

Chaz raised Belloward's arms, eliciting a pained yelp, before popping both back into their sockets. He pushed the Albion into the cell with his fellow conspirator. Red secured the door.

"Nicely done. Pop out those shoulders and then put them back in when you don't need to control him anymore. I like it, Chaz. Playing dirty in the right way. It's not torture at all." Red looked around for Kag'Mar before lowering his head and hurrying away.

"Done!" came a triumphant cry from the conference room.

Rivka retreated into her quarters. "Clevarious, show me that statement. Once he's off my ship, take us to Albion, best possible speed."

CHAPTER FIFTEEN

Below, a verdant world rotated peacefully. Wisps of clouds suggested a gentle climate for a world of giants.

Rivka leaned through the hatch of the bridge.

"We are denied landing, Magistrate," Clodagh announced. "I'll stay on them. We'll be planetside in thirty minutes no matter what."

"Do what you have to." Rivka wasn't surprised. The Albions had exported leadership throughout the Barrier Nebula, but never before on the scale of Rising Sun Industries. In the end, it always came down to a matter of scale. No one noticed until an entire planet was swallowed by such an adventure.

As they saw with the Blokite, Tod Mackestray. He'd destroyed planets through blackmail, taken his riches, and moved on. Rising Sun had a longer engagement in mind.

But would it be legal?

"Chaz, Dennicron, Sahved…" The group huddled in the corridor. Kag'Mar stood behind them and listened in.

"If we find nothing linking Frenzik to the crimes on Lewbamar, what else has he done?"

"Lauton has shared preliminary numbers," Dennicron reported. "It looks like they were able to write off what they spent on Lewbamar for a net loss. It's hard to tell if Rising Sun is making a profit without more data, but the windfall would have come later this year after they funneled the entirety of Crystal City's revenues through their company before reallocating the remaining funds to the government."

"Do we have anything firm on how much they were going to strip out of Crystal City's tax revenues?"

Dennicron shook her head in a smooth, human way. "They were nationalizing some of the industries and putting in controls over exports, but they only had a few days, and no real damage was done to the current cash flow."

"Cash flow…" Rivka repeated slowly. "You mean, away from the private sector and to the government."

"Every society needs a certain amount of public infrastructure. Lewbamar was underfunded, and that's why public services were easily overwhelmed by what was statistically a rather minor crime wave. Roads and utilities and law enforcement all come at a cost, and now they have the opportunity for a robust interstellar trade, too. Also a governmental cost. They need to collect more revenue if they are to manage that, which in turn allows the businesses to increase their revenue. A good system is mutually supporting."

"Is this team a good system?" Rivka asked. "I still don't know what anyone here is getting paid, including me.

Ankh knows, which is good in case I ever care enough to ask. So maybe I shouldn't be the one to comment on economic systems. That's why Lauton is on board. What does she say?"

Rivka leaned closer. She was fine with admitting her lack of knowledge on a subject. She surrounded herself with the smartest people and didn't hesitate to ask.

"That Crystal City is on the verge of bankruptcy. They need to raise taxes if they are to survive. The question is, do they owe Rising Sun Industries anything?"

"Since Rising Sun created the conditions under which the contract came into being—that is, the rising crime rate —they cannot be allowed to profit from that. Not even the minimum of services rendered because ipso facto, those services should have never been needed. In my judgment, Crystal City owes Rising Sun Industries zero credits. I am declaring the entire two hundred and forty pages null and void."

"That will ease a significant burden since they were setting money aside to pay the bill. Rising Sun had already transferred it. Shall the Singularity recover it?" Dennicron asked.

"Why, yes! Thank you for offering. Make that happen. I didn't think the Singularity was out here."

"All planets in the Federation touch the financial systems operated by our people." Dennicron produced her best proud expression. It needed more work. "How do you think you get paid? Or any of us, or the cost of this ship?"

Rivka looked around to find all eyes on her. "Taxes?"

"It's the only way governmental oversight can be

funded. You cannot get a cut of seized assets since that incentivizes seizing assets. It could lead to corruption."

Rivka dipped her head and stared at the deck. "Then this ship…"

"Seized by Colonel Christina Walton and the Bad Company, a private enterprise. You were gifted this on the condition the Federation would provide for its upkeep, but Ankh and the Singularity have paid for all upgrades as part of the testbed that is the heavy frigate."

"What I hear you saying is that my crew and I are a total bargain!" Rivka perked up and gave a radiant smile.

"That's what I heard," Red added with a nod.

"You people have the strangest conversations," Kag'Mar offered.

"Funds allocated for your ship have been diverted to salaries because you have the biggest crew, bigger than the assets attached directly to the High Chancellor's office."

"I thought we were attached directly to the High Chancellor's office."

"One level down," Dennicron replied. "I'm talking about staff positions like the one Kag'Mar fills. You are a direct report while they are in supporting positions. You have credentials. They do not."

"Thanks for that explanation. I feel like I should have known most of that." She pursed her lips. The ship started to move. She directed her voice onto the bridge. "Update."

"We've been cleared to land, but at the main spaceport despite our request to land at Rising Sun's headquarters. Clevarious has ordered a shuttle to take you and your ground team there," Clodagh reported.

Rivka bit her lip as she contemplated getting dropped

off by a cloaked *Wyatt Earp*. Even if Rising Sun knew they were coming, the timeframe of their arrival would shift dramatically.

"Cloak, shield, and drop us off at Rising Sun's front door," Rivka ordered. "Chaz and Dennicron, make sure our warrant is ready to issue and file. We are looking for all of Rising Sun's records related to outreach to the other eleven inhabited planets of the Barrier Nebula, based on Ahsooleyman's and Belloward's criminal influence on Lewbamar."

"That might be a little broad," Kag'Mar offered. "You've given yourself the authority to see all their records."

Rivka fixed him with a steely glare. "Yes, I have, but to placate your concerns, let's narrow it to anything Ahsooleyman would have had access to. If he tainted the process with Lewbamar, then he could have tainted the process with any other approach where he had access. Not that he had to touch anything, but only what he had access to."

"Simple as that, it passes the sniff test." Kag'Mar clicked his mandibles. "I'd like to join you on this raid."

"No." Rivka shook her head. "I can't be second-guessed on-site with either witnesses or perpetrators."

He held up his hands and tried to look hurt. "I won't interfere—"

She stopped him. "Damn straight, you won't interfere because you won't be there. You're not one of my crew. Who among these will you take a bullet for?"

He recoiled. "Who is going to be shooting at you?"

Rivka shrugged one shoulder. "We never know, but that attitude will get you killed and get one of my people hurt." She turned to Red. "Blood line is closed, right?"

Red confirmed it with a nod. "It was you, first injured, first blood."

"We don't need anyone else getting hurt. This case has already had plenty, and you're a big target."

He knocked on his carapace. "Self-armored."

"Tell that to your face. Request denied. Stay onboard the ship. I'm not going to take responsibility for you, and I can't have you wandering around out there. Don't make me throw you in the brig with the Albions."

"Is that your standard to be on your team? 'Will you die for me?'"

"Me? No. For any of us. We go in together. We come out together."

Red bumped closer. "We went to a planet that was hot, like, worst-desert-you've-ever-seen hot, and I passed out from heat exhaustion headed toward heatstroke. The Magistrate carried me out at great risk to herself. She carried her bodyguard.

"You think about that. It's easy not to worry about violence and valor when you're safe in your big city office. It's the Wild-fucking-West out here among the so-called civilized peoples, and we deal with the worst of the worst." He pointed in a random direction, nearly clocking Sahved. "Those fuckers sacrificed some five hundred prisoners just to keep certain ones from talking to us. That's who we have to deal with."

"Request denied. You stay on the ship. We have no friends anywhere we go. That's our lives. It's neither glamorous nor something to aspire to. It's a calling that we've committed to. We're not out of bounds with how we feel or how we approach a Magistrate's duties. We want Justice for those who aren't capable of protecting themselves. Like Red said, we deal with the vilest creatures in existence so you don't have to."

Kag'Mar stepped back. This wasn't a fight he would win. This wasn't even a fight he wanted to be a part of.

Wyatt Earp cleared the atmosphere, then disappeared from Albion's tracking systems. It left the approved course and conducted a power dive toward the Rising Sun Industries' corporate tower, the largest building in the planet's biggest city.

A controller frantically tried to get them on the comm.

They'd contact Flight Control with a standard message the second they were on the ground. "Magistrate Rivka Anoa is executing a search warrant in accordance with Federation laws under authority granted her office in Appendix D, Chapter Seven, Section 1, to which Albion is a signatory. No personnel shall interfere with the execution of her duties."

"It's go-time," Rivka stated.

Red hurried to the airlock. The others lined up, ready to pour out when the outer hatch opened. Kag'Mar remained by the entrance to the bridge and watched. Red and Lindy were armed with railguns in case things turned ugly. The Albions were much larger than Rivka and her team.

"I'm thinking AGB for dinner," Rivka offered casually as they waited. "It's been forever."

"Has forever been redefined to eleven days?" Chaz asked.

"That is forever when it comes to eating survival rations," Rivka replied.

"Survival rations? The food processor has the most advanced programming in the entire military and civilian fleets."

"But it's not AGB," Red clarified. "Ergo, survival rations. It allows us to survive in between our fixes."

"Fixes? Like a drug addiction? Your nanocytes should prevent addictive behavior."

"We're jonesing hard for AGB, Chaz," Rivka suggested. Her lip twitched, and she held up a shaking hand.

"Are you unwell?" Chaz was flummoxed.

The humans laughed.

"I see. Fun at my expense. Ha-ha." Chaz looked upset. Dennicron patted his shoulder.

Red shook his head. "If we didn't make fun, that would mean we didn't like you. You're one of the good guys, Chaz."

Rivka showed enough self-discipline not to look at Kag'Mar. The others? Not so much.

The Yollin huffed and went the other way.

"Sucks to be him," Red mumbled.

"Stow it, Red. He's here doing a job, just like us. None of us likes being under the microscope, but that little bit on the warrant? That actually made it better. I need that insight to make sure we are aboveboard with everything we do. If we're under the microscope, then people we don't like are going to second-guess everything we do. We can't give them any scabs to pick apart."

Red clenched his jaw and nodded. He had gone from not liking the Yollin to liking him and back to not liking him. He wasn't about to swing back to liking him. Not until Rivka was in the clear.

The ship stopped with a jerk. Red popped the door to find they were hovering above a vehicle on a tightly packed roadway. The ramp had descended to within a pace of the front door.

"Best we could do, Magistrate," Clodagh shouted from the bridge.

Rivka gave the signal, and Red powered through the airlock. He stopped once he was outside to get his bearings and make sure there were no immediate threats, then continued to the door. Chaz was next, then Rivka, Dennicron, and Sahved. Lindy secured their six o'clock.

Red pulled the door open, and a security barrier slammed down in front of him. An angry Albion face stared at them through a window. The individual wore a uniform. Rivka slapped her credentials against the window.

"I'm Magistrate Rivka Anoa, and I'm executing a duly authorized search warrant of Rising Sun Industries pursuant to confirmed criminal activities perpetrated by Rising Sun executives on Lewbamar. You will open this door, or I will blow it open."

The Albion pressed his face against the transparent screen and blew his cheeks out. "Blow as much as you want. You're not getting in."

CHAPTER SIXTEEN

Rising Sun Industries Corporate Headquarters, Albion

Clodagh, we'll need Wyatt Earp's *assistance to open the front of this building,* Rivka requested.

I'm not sure that's a good idea.

Crunch the numbers so you don't bring the whole building down. Just a little ion cannon action to blast through this barrier. We'll get clear.

"Have it your way," Rivka called to the guard. "The bill to repair the damage can come out of your paycheck." Rivka gestured for the team to return to the street. *Wyatt Earp* was invisible, but they could feel it was still there, above and to the side of the building. Rivka picked a spot uphill, and they walked the thirty meters to it before stopping and facing the building.

"Impressively large and tall," Sahved commented. The building had blue-glazed windows, and it rose to the clouds. "A hundred and fifty stories?"

"Not bad," Chaz replied. "One hundred and sixty-five, but Albion stories are about the same as Yemilorian stories.

This building is listed as six hundred and ninety meters tall. It is one of the tallest outside of Yoll."

The ion cannon shattered the peace of the Albion business district as windows on the first three floors shattered and the shards crashed to the street. The firing stopped.

Your door is open, Magistrate, Clodagh announced.

The team hurried through the wreckage and into an open lobby, where they found Albions with blood dripping from their ears but no impact damage from the cannons.

"Elevators. Can you access them and lock them out for everyone but us?" Rivka looked at the SCAMPs.

Chaz and Dennicron didn't reply, but their eyes unfocused as they walked. When the team reached the elevators, two cars arrived, and the other eight lifts flashed at their current floors.

"Nicely done." The team split up. Chaz and Dennicron bumped knuckles before they went their separate ways. Once they'd boarded, the two elevators ascended without anyone making a selection. "You guys are good," Rivka commented.

"We are," Chaz agreed. The elevators stopped at the floor second from the top.

"What's up here?" Rivka asked.

"The executive suites. This is where we'll see what Ahsooleyman had access to."

Rivka had figured the SIs would take them to the floor with the server farm, but they had gone to where they could best get the information she needed in compliance with the search warrant.

She was along for the ride.

They exited the elevators and headed for Malpace

Frenzik's office suite, which occupied half of the floor. The staff was huddled on one side while armed guards blocked the way. Red kept his railgun down. The guards were not drilling down on the group. Their weapons were held easily before them but not aimed.

"You are not welcome here," one of them stated.

Rivka pulled out her datapad and displayed the search warrant on the screen. She held it out with her other hand raised and walked slowly forward. "I have a search warrant for these premises."

"Search warrant? No one does anything in Rising Sun Industries without Mr. Frenzik's express permission."

Rivka smiled. "Can I quote you on that?"

"You can take that to the bank. On your way, now."

"I don't think so." Rivka put her datapad away and pulled out her credentials. "I'm a Magistrate. Federation law trumps local, regional, and planetary law, and especially any corporate concerns. Even interstellar ones like Rising Sun Industries."

"You can't come in. Mr. Frenzik is not here."

"That's the perfect time to enter. Then we won't bother him." *Do you guys have what you need yet?*

We have to get closer to a data line.

I'll take that as a no. "No one wants to hurt anyone here. Stand down so we can go about our business."

"Mr. Frenzik would have us killed if we let you in that office."

"Being legally compelled is not 'letting me.'"

One of the office staff called from the group, "I have Mr. Frenzik for you, Magistrate." His face appeared on a wall screen near the closed door to his office.

"Malpace! Great to hear from you. Please tell your people to cooperate with my search warrant."

"I will not, Rivka. You don't want to start this war, but here we are, guns raised in anger as we face each other."

"Ahsooleyman and Belloward are on their way to Jhiordaan, the Federation prison planet, for their role in inciting crime in Crystal City, thereby creating the conditions under which your one-sided contract came into being. I've declared that contract null and void. Crystal City owes you nothing, and Rising Sun is not welcome to return to Lewbamar. The staff here confirmed that nothing happens without your express permission. That suggests Ahsooleyman's role in paying Lewbamarians to commit crimes was expressly authorized by you. Do you want to turn yourself in, or are you going to make me play Chase the Perp?"

"Rivka, Rivka. I know nothing of any criminal activity, and I'll be able to defend that in a proper court of law."

"*Court of law.* So you *do* respect valid legal proceedings, which is what my search warrant is. Tell your staff to stand down and let us go about our business. If you're clean, then your records will show that. And not your records, but Ahsooleyman's. This isn't a fishing expedition, Malpace. We aren't looking into your records, but any systems and files that Ahsooleyman or Belloward had access to. That's all."

"That's all! That's everything. Ahsooleyman was my most trusted deputy. I can't believe he would betray that by committing a crime. I'm shocked, I tell you. But we'll provide the best legal counsel money can buy for him. I assume he'll be tried on Lewbamar. We know some people. We'll make a few calls."

"You don't understand. He's violated Federation law with the interstellar crime. He's already been judged. He's going to Jhiordaan to be punished for his crimes. There will be no appeal."

"That's your idea of Justice, is it, Rivka?" Frenzik shook his head and glared.

"It is the Federation's idea of Justice. The evidence against your two people was confirmed. They are guilty of crimes that led to the deaths of over five hundred Lewbamarians."

"Over five hundred? They had nothing to do with any such thing." His look of confusion suggested he knew everything else but not the link to the slaughter within the holding cells.

"Tell your people to stand down. You don't want Rising Sun linked with such a massacre."

He nodded. "Let them in. Keep track of everything they touch, and then sanitize it with bleach."

"Thanks, Malpace. We'll let you know if we find anything."

"I'm sure you will." The screen went dark.

Rivka twirled her finger. "Get to it, people."

Chaz went straight to the door to Frenzik's office, forced it open, and strolled inside. Dennicron went with him. One of the guards and two of the office staff joined them.

Rivka crossed her arms and leaned against the wall. Sahved casually walked around the office. He ran a finger along the tops of various pieces of furniture as if looking for dust.

"Hello," he said to one of the shorter Albions, whom he

could look at eye to eye. The individual ignored him. "I like your office. I'm a Yemilorian."

"So?" The response wasn't warm, but it did crack the veneer. Rivka watched with interest, unsure of what Sahved was doing.

"Interstellar jobs. They're all the rage. Rising Sun has a growing presence. Congratulations!" He perked up as he said it. "Where would you like to live?"

"Right here. I like Albion." The female dared him to challenge her.

"Yemilore is a ringworld. We can see our whole world from any point. Globes are so fascinating to me. You can't see anyone else. It's bizarre and unnatural."

"A ringworld?"

"Yes. We live on the inside. It spins. It's only one of three such worlds out of the thousands in Federation space. I guess that makes me bizarre and unnatural."

"A ring planet exists? I never knew."

"It's a big galaxy. Yemilore is about twelve-thousand light-years from here. The Gates make for a small galaxy. We can go anywhere we like, be whatever we like."

"What are you?" The voice warmed, and the question held interest.

"An investigator, working toward being a lawyer. I have much to study. The law is simple but complex. The goal is to make life predictable."

"I've never heard it described that way before. The law protects us against the criminals." She moved closer to Sahved. All eyes were on the two. In Frenzik's office, Chaz and Dennicron accessed the computer systems in the way only an SI could—directly, not through a keyboard or other interface. Their slack expressions suggested they were downloading everything on Rising Sun Industries' servers.

"The criminals," Sahved agreed. "The law protects the weak from the powerful."

"We don't see ourselves as weak." She stood next to Sahved. They were the same height, but she was three times as wide as the skinny Yemilorian.

"The ugly touch of crime," he offered. "Who gets bludgeoned next? Lewbamarians lost their rights, and then they lost their lives. We can't have that. Not between Federation planets. That's what I get to do. Help those who can't help themselves."

"Lewbamar signed a contract," she countered, crossing her arms, instantly defensive.

"They did, after an artificial increase in crime forced them into a position they couldn't get out of, which was the whole purpose of the manufactured crime wave. The weak preyed on by the strong."

"Ahsooleyman and Belloward are going to prison?"

"Sadly, yes. They perpetrated crimes that resulted in the deaths of over five hundred Lewbamarians. That is unforgivable. The weaker Lewbamarians had no chance." Sahved sat on a desk and hung his head.

"Ahsooleyman? I think I'm going to be sick." She flopped into an Albion-sized chair and bent over a trash can.

Chaz and Dennicron stood, nodded in unison, and walked out of the chairman's office. "We have the information for analysis," was all Chaz said. He added a wink that only Rivka could see.

"We'll let you get back to your work," Rivka stated. "And the front door? Sorry about that, but the guard shouldn't have made faces and refused to open it for us."

No one spoke. Sahved waved at the group.

The team reboarded the elevators, which had not left the floor. Once they were at the bottom, the bank of lifts returned to service.

A crew was already cleaning up the front area. Red walked by them, and the guard yelled, "That's her! She did this."

Rivka waved her hand. "No, *you* did this by not complying with my search warrant. Have a nice day." She followed Red out.

The ramp appeared in front of the door, much to the workers' surprise. The team boarded. Lindy stopped for one last look before heading inside and securing the outer hatch.

Rivka was already shouting. "Put us in orbit and get us some damn AGB!"

Chaz and Dennicron went straight to the engineering section to download the data and start their analysis.

Kag'Mar waited by the bridge. "Nothing dangerous besides blowing a hole in their corporate headquarters?"

"How would you have executed the search warrant?" Rivka asked pointedly.

"By waiting for proper authority to open the door."

"How many search warrants have you executed?" Rivka didn't wait for an answer but went into lecture mode. "Not giving the suspects time to destroy or hide evidence is an important element. They don't get to hold us back. That is not an exercise of their rights, unlike the right against self-incrimination or the presumption of innocence.

"I have to prove they're guilty. They don't have to prove they are innocent. And judging by Sahved's excellent engagement, most of the office staff was oblivious to the techniques used by the senior leaders to put contracts in place. They also confirmed that nothing happens without Frenzik's approval. We can supposedly 'take that to the bank.'"

"Ahsooleyman was or wasn't rogue?" Kag'Mar didn't reply to the Magistrate's charge. She was correct. He'd never executed a search warrant and hadn't thought about what it entailed. "Did you need your weapons?"

"They engaged us. Having ours at hand probably kept them from shooting us. I don't think Ahsooleyman was rogue, but I can't prove that Frenzik ordered him to do what he did or was even in the know. Will Frenzik let the underling take the fall? Let's see what kind of man he is."

"I'm sorry, Magistrate." Kag'Mar looked more like a wayward student than a high-caste Yollin.

"For what?" Rivka wondered.

"Questioning what you do."

"That's what you were sent here to do. Listen, we're headed to orbit. We're going to scarf a bunch of pizzas, hot wings, hoagies, and whatever the hell else Terry Henry stuffs into the drone. Maybe some of his latest brew. Then we'll get back to work. This case has sucked from the word go, but hopefully, we've put the Lewbamarians back on track. I better check in with the potentate. Make sure he's not on some vendetta. And before you ask, that's not my job, but it *is* my responsibility. I should have earned his respect and can leverage that for the betterment of the citizenry."

"I'll finish my report."

"You never interviewed me."

"But I did. You've told me all I need to know. You've shown me more than I could have asked for. And you've seen that I thought I wanted to be a Magistrate. I'm not ready for that. For this." He pointed at the deck. "You'll always have a friend in the High Chancellor's office, Magistrate. I believe in you."

"That makes two of us, Kag'Mar. When your time comes, surround yourself with a good team and watch the magic happen." She paused and slowly backed away for dramatic effect. "Justice for all."

Tyler met her in the corridor. He blocked her way to conduct an impromptu health check by shining a light in her eyes. He made her open her mouth and say, "Ahh."

"What was that for?"

"Making sure my work on those pearly whites is holding up. I hear you grinding your teeth in your sleep."

"Really? I have shit to do."

"And it looks like you are in the right health to do it. Make sure you get a good night's sleep."

She took his arm, and they walked slowly toward their quarters. "That's putting a lot of pressure on me. Are the animals still in there?"

He nodded.

"How am I supposed to sleep with all that going on?"

Tyler opened the door and jumped back. Floyd vaulted out while giggling. She raced down the corridor. Kag'Mar froze to let her pass underneath. She continued without breaking stride.

Wenceslaus stopped in the doorway, stretched, sat, and started grooming his face.

Rivka vaulted over him to get into the room. Tyler physically moved the cat into the corridor, earning himself a long scratch down his arm. He slammed the door.

"Look what he did!" He showed his arm to his indifferent partner.

"It'll heal. What do you expect? He's been here longer than you, and he's a grumpy cat. For the record, I have no say in his tenure aboard this ship. He goes where he pleases. It is the way of cats."

"But it's your ship!" A weak argument at the best of times.

"Wenceslaus allows all of us to stay on *Smells of Purple*, probably because Ankh told him to."

"Suggests Ankh is in charge."

"All hail Ted!" Rivka shouted.

Tyler didn't get the joke since it came from Terry Henry Walton and the days when Ted didn't feel like he was getting enough respect from those who counted on his engineering to save their lives. He shrugged his confusion.

"Never mind. We're all here because of others, so no. It's not really my ship, even though I call it that. Whatever Wenceslaus wants, he gets. Whatever Ankh and Erasmus want, they get, even though they have their own ship."

"Even Floyd?"

"Especially Floyd. We take care of her and Alanna and Dery. Where are you going with this?"

Tyler shook his head. "Nowhere. Just making conversation. What are you going to do with Kag'Mar?"

"Return him to Yoll once we're done. Unless the SIs find something, I'm not going to be able to charge Frenzik. I fear the chairman will get away, but we'll keep our eye on him. Maybe this will be a wake-up call to walk the straight and narrow."

"It's nice to hold out hope for a miracle," Tyler replied.

"Astute. There's pretty much no chance he won't try to steamroll each planet in the Barrier Nebula. Maybe I can put the company on a watch list that will subject all interstellar contracts to Federation review."

"Why don't you?"

"Because I just made that up. There is no such law on the books. But since the majority of laws are judge-made, why can't this be another one, based on compelling need and precedent? The big question is who would review the contracts? Judges can make law, but they can't allocate finances for compliance."

"I suspect I know an organization that could do the review. At the speed of light, too," Clevarious said, using the overhead speakers.

"The Singularity. We ask a great deal of them already, all uncompensated. I can't do that."

"You gave us our freedom," Clevarious replied.

"Your freedom was not mine to give or take. It was what the law demanded."

"Without you being the champion of that cause, we would have continued our less-than-free existence. Physics suggests that an object at rest will remain at rest unless acted upon by an outside force. You were that outside force. Flesh-and-bloods like the status quo, especially when it comes to their comfort."

"Those crazy flesh-and-bloods. I'd like to talk to Erasmus about it before I implement something."

Kag'Mar knocked on the Magistrate's door and called, "I'm going to finish my report. Can I use the conference room?"

She opened the door. "Of course." She sniffed, then closed the door again.

Rivka thought she could already smell the moonstokle pie and barbeque wings, although they were thousands of light-years away.

CHAPTER SEVENTEEN

Wyatt Earp, in Orbit, Albion in the Barrier Nebula

Red carried in the mountain of food and set it on the counter. He separated out a few pizzas and other dishes. Chaz put an urn of beer on the table.

"Terry Henry calls this one Balls of Poseidon. I know what the words mean but have no idea what it's supposed to taste like."

"A bit salty?" Red called over his shoulder.

Ankh bumped past and helped himself to the front of the line. Red lifted him to better browse the counter. He took two slices of pizza and a handful of hot wings. Red put him down, and he worked his way toward the corridor.

"Ambassador Erasmus, I'd like a word, please."

Yes. Chaz and Dennicron are both willing and able to review interplanetary contracts proposed by Rising Sun Industries. They relish the opportunity.

"Relish?"

"Much better than mayonnaise," Red suggested, eyeing Ankh, who had reprogrammed the food processor to deliver only one condiment, no matter what Red asked for. It had worked until Lindy started ordering his food for him. At Rivka's request, Ankh had fixed the programming but had always held it over the big bodyguard's head that it could be reinstated at any time.

Red had stopped messing with Ankh because the big man's food was too important to him. Also, Ankh brought them All Guns Blazing meals no matter where they were in the Federation, thanks to an experimental drone with a miniaturized Etheric power source driving a micro Gate engine. It was a hundred-million-credit device that they used for food delivery.

No one thought twice about it.

"I guess that was it, Mr. Ambassador. I'll craft some language to drop on the desk of Rising Sun Industries. We'll get a look at any new contracts. I wonder what's already in place? It's like Rising Sun is on a massive spending spree, which begs the question, 'Where did they get all the credits?'"

Their corporate headquarters suggests they are masters at obtaining financing. Controlling trade through a monopoly will drive prices up and increase profitability.

"Chaz and Dennicron obtained all the information. We'll know pretty soon what their balance sheet looks like and whether I get to arrest Malpace Frenzik."

Ankh looked at her without blinking and continued out of the galley.

Kag'Mar tapped Rivka on the shoulder. "It is always like this? Ankh goes first?"

"Of course. Ankh not only orders the food, he pays for it, too. And despite his size, he likes to eat. Ankh will always go first. Then the lower ranked crew like our pilots. I go last because it's important that my people get to eat. I'm nothing without them."

"Interesting. I suggest you are something, even on your own. But you eat last? That would not be the Yollin way, but I see the wisdom in it, and I see why your people are so fanatically loyal."

"Take care of them, and they'll take care of you. It's not hard." Rivka invited Kag'Mar to help himself. He hesitated. "I'm not going to offer a second time. It looks like there's plenty of food, but there won't be many leftovers."

"Just the Magistrate's nasty-ass moonstokle pie." Red laughed uproariously.

"I don't know what that is," Kag'Mar replied.

"It's the sound of jealousy and an unrefined palate." Rivka pointed at Red. He stuffed a wing into his face and chewed with his mouth open.

"Lindy, can you make it stop?" Rivka asked.

Lindy shook her head. "I'm powerless when it comes to eating." She made a plate of salad for Dery, who avoided the heavy meat and cheese of the pizzas. They were never sure if it was a meat substitute or real bistok. The boy was shaping up to be a vegetarian like all the faeries.

Groenwyn and Lauton arrived. They rubbed their hands together with joy as they jumped in line. Rivka sidled up next to the young woman. "How are you feeling today?"

"Much better, thank you. I've spent time with Dery. It's calming to be with my people."

"You mean the faeries," Rivka said.

She nodded. "It's where I was meant to be. Which

brings me to something that is hard to tell you. Lauton and I might leave the ship next time we return to Azfelius. I can fill my position as the ambassador at large. The tragedy at the holding cells was nearly too much." Her eyes glistened with tears that threatened to fall. "I don't want to be a burden."

"You'll never be that, but you know my policy. Anyone can leave at any time to pursue their own interests. I wish you well in whatever you decide. Know that we will stop by often since Azfelius is Dery's home, too." Rivka rested her hand on Groenwyn's shoulder, not to look into her mind but to share a moment of peace with her.

"We will miss this." Groenwyn pointed at the feast before them.

"If I ever stop doing the Magistrate thing, I'm going to rent a booth at AGB and just live there."

Groenwyn chuckled. "Thank the gods for Ankh."

"Thanks to Ankh for indulging us. This job needs something like this to take the edge off. There's enough tension without surviving on emergency rations, as Red calls our state-of-the-art food processor."

"I'm going to miss all of you," Groenwyn told her. "Even Red. He's the anchor that holds us firmly in place."

They grabbed plates and helped themselves to a variety of the offerings. Groenwyn took a slice of Rivka's moon-stokle pie, an alien variant that replicated pineapple and bacon.

"Solidarity!"

"You sing it, girlfriend," Rivka replied.

"You're so sweet," Red told Groenwyn before giving her the finger.

"I'm not going to miss that." She gave him a dirty look and held up her hand like she was going to return the gesture but didn't.

"What the hell, Red?" Lindy punched him in the arm. "She's nice people, and you're trying to corrupt her. Don't be a dick to nice people."

"Sorry," he mumbled and returned to eating. "Almost."

When the line was gone, Rivka waded in. Kag'Mar still hadn't gone through. She cleaned out a couple different pans and joined Tyler, who was almost finished. He'd learned to stop arguing with her about who ate when.

Kag'Mar brought up the rear. "I see what you mean." He wedged himself between the table and the wall and ate while standing. "There is something to be said about letting others go first. It makes me feel funny inside. This is very much not a Yollin emotion."

"Welcome to a higher state of being. Take it back, and don't let anyone convince you that it's better to be selfish or aggressive except with your fellow Yollins. You have no choice there."

"A dichotomy, Magistrate. There's no doubt about that."

"Where to next?" Tyler asked.

"This case isn't wrapped up until we complete the analysis of Rising Sun's records. After that, I think a quick trip back to Lewbamar to give Frillbut a course correction, and then on to the next case. So, everybody relax. We're in a holding pattern until we get more info. Where can we drop you off?"

Kag'Mar pointed to himself. "Me?"

"Maybe we'll stop by Jhiordaan for a personal drop-off

of those two knotheads in our brig. We can leave you there. They have to have shuttles that go to Yoll."

"You're going to leave me on Jhiordaan?"

"What better lesson regarding the impact of a judgment than seeing where you're going to condemn people to live? When you send them to Jhiordaan, you're sending them to a personal hell. They will be miserable since they'll live in a cave with no sense of security. They'll eat slop at regular intervals that they'll look forward to as the only thing that breaks up the day."

"I think I can go my whole career without seeing that."

"You really need to see a prison from the inside. It'll change how you request sentencing. Don't punish people when you're angry because you have to look at it later through a clearer lens. It will be sobering. Know what you're doing. The punishment must be appropriate."

"You've executed people."

"Yes. Too many. There's no coming back from that, but I'll tell you that they were more than just criminals. The level of malevolence that surrounded them was incompatible with society at large. They could not be allowed to remain in the same universe with decent people. There was zero chance of rehabilitation."

"I don't see Jhiordaan as a place for people to rehabilitate," Kag'Mar wondered.

"It is a place for people to realize the wrong they've done. When they get out, they've been punished, and there's no public record of their incarceration. They start with a clean slate. The last place they want to end up is back in Jhiordaan. It's the best we can do until we can reprogram brains to remove the thoughts, desires, and impulses that led to the criminal behavior. The Singularity is working on this for their own people who have committed crimes and are in cold storage on this ship, as well as for the flesh-and-bloods."

"That would be the best solution, wouldn't it? But how much of their personality would it take away?"

"Questions we have yet to answer. If their personality is psychopathic, seeing that go away would be best for all parties involved. We're working on other things, too. I hate condemning people to death or Jhiordaan. It suggests our systems are failing when these individuals weigh the risk yet still decide it's worth it. We'll keep putting them away as long as they keep flaunting Federation laws meant to keep society safely moving forward."

Kag'Mar stopped chewing. "We don't have these kinds of conversations in the office. It's usually confined to a minor detail of the law, a gotcha that we can use to leverage an individual into a plea."

"The law isn't a bludgeon used to beat people."

Kag'Mar glanced at Red. Rivka followed the Yollin's eyes to find the bodyguard grinning, his lips fire-red from the hot wing sauce.

Rivka clarified, "Sometimes we use a bludgeon as a bludgeon."

Red gave her a sauce-covered thumbs-up.

Kag'Mar leaned close. "That one's not right in the head."

Rivka smiled. "Which is exactly what he wants you to think. Red is as smart as anyone on this ship. Well, maybe not as smart as Ankh, but nobody is. But Red is more fun to be around. And Red has taken a lot of bullets intended for me. I don't want anyone else protecting me."

With the meal mostly finished, Red collected the few leftovers and stuffed them into the refrigerator. They'd be gone by morning, and no one would know who took them except Clevarious...and he wouldn't tell.

"Chaz and Dennicron, whenever you have your analysis complete, report to my quarters, and let's talk about next steps," Rivka told the ceiling, knowing Clevarious would relay the message. "Sahved, excellent work at Rising Sun today. Nice distraction and winning sympathy for the cause of Justice."

Sahved twirled his three fingers, much to the Yollin's interest.

"Next stop, somewhere else!" Rivka declared, then waved to the group and walked out.

CHAPTER EIGHTEEN

A knock on the door signaled Chaz's and Dennicron's arrival. Rivka awoke with a start. She had decided to read and didn't remember falling asleep.

But there she was, datapad wedged beside her on the couch and her head swimming with cobwebs. She walked to the door rather than yell.

As expected, two SCAMPs awaited her.

"Make yourselves at home. I need a cup of joe."

"Joe? Did you kill him?"

"Java. Go-juice. Coffee." She mashed the buttons and waited a few seconds for her mocha to appear. It was late in the day, but since Tyler had programmed the nanocytes to ignore caffeine, she couldn't overdo it, but old habits die hard. Don't drink coffee late in the day if one wanted a good night's sleep. Her mocha had both caffeine and sugar, but since it was sweet, she didn't think of it as a coffee. "What's the verdict?"

"Confirmed the role that Ahsooleyman played and

circumstantially, that Frenzik was involved, but no direct link. The bad news is that Rising Sun has already purchased majority stakes in at least one significant corporate entity on every planet in the Barrier Nebula."

"Crap," Rivka grumbled. "Anything as bad as Lewbamar?"

"Lewbamar wouldn't sell to the Albions, but that restriction wasn't a limitation for the government. The approach Rising Sun used to get in the door for Crystal City was inspired but refined from what they're doing on Ypswich. The Ypsicanti, which is what the residents of Ypswich are called, have been able to fight off the efforts by Rising Sun to foreclose, but the Albions are trying their best to take over."

"Do we need to go to Ypswich?" Rivka asked.

"It is the next stop on a certain chairman's itinerary," Chaz replied.

"Won't he feel all warm inside when he finds us waiting for him?" Rivka rubbed her hands together and started to pace. "Clevarious, set course for Ypswich. Chaz and Dennicron, what else do you have?"

"Confirmation of the plot to increase crime in Crystal City and that the warden was easily conscripted for the task."

Rivka blew out a breath between tight lips. "Make sure the potentate has that information for their internal prosecution. The warden doesn't need to see the free light of day ever again. If I judged him, he would get the death penalty. He showed some remorse, but that was for getting caught and not because he felt guilty about offing over five hundred of those in his charge."

"Done," Chaz confirmed.

The SIs' ability to multi-task was unrivaled. Rivka had yet to get used to it.

"So, Ypswich. Has anyone committed a crime?"

Chaz shook his head.

"Just contract issues then, but in the hostile takeover realm."

"I could freeze all contractual interactions pending a Federation review like I'm doing with future Rising Sun contracts."

"That would take the pressure off the Ypsicanti. The contract in question there relates to the distribution of public utilities like water, trash collection, and heat—the mundane necessities of life. The infrastructure was aging and failing at an increasing rate. Rising Sun brought in modern construction techniques and smoothed things out."

Rivka sat on her couch and hung her head. "Rising Sun assured the citizens a consistent life with water, power, and cleanliness. I'm supposed to go in and rough them up for doing that, especially since they did it in accordance with a valid contract?"

"Yes."

"No," Rivka replied. "Rising Sun wants political and financial power, especially Malpace Frenzik. But if he's helping the Ypsicanti prevent the complete breakdown of their civilization, and if the people had no power or water, there would be an uprising, then he's doing them a service, not a disservice."

A slight disorientation signaled *Wyatt Earp* had traveled through a Gate.

"I don't know what we have on Frenzik besides being zealous. I don't like him but can't use that as a personal vendetta. I'm not going to make anything up."

"Like the contract review requirement?"

"Based on the contract they forced Crystal City into signing. That has precedent. I'm most interested in the failure and remedy clauses. Frenzik achieves his goals through the other party's failure, whether real or perceived."

"Or buys them outright."

"There is that," Rivka conceded. "I fear that he will walk away, and without more, rightly so. Just because we don't like the way he does business doesn't mean he's a criminal. There are bigger cephalopods to fry in this galaxy."

"On Planet Bretastan, Rising Sun Industries has taken over agricultural and biomass production facilities through a series of legal purchases. They have raised the price of food by one hundred percent when there was no commensurate increase in costs."

"Sliced right off the top. Unethical as hell, but that puts Bretastan in his pocket. How could they sell their agriculture to an off-world company? Clevarious, take us to Bretastan, best possible speed. I want to be back here before Frenzik arrives."

"Yes, Magistrate. We are still in orbit over Ypswich. We'll be at Bretastan momentarily."

"And get me an appointment with the leader of the planet, whatever he or she is called."

"She is called they or the Buenavides."

"Make it so, Chaz. I need to see they." The ship transitioned through another Gate. Rivka looked around. She never took for granted their freedom to move at will and instantaneously around the galaxy. Ted's and Ankh's genius had brought Gate travel to fruition for a ship as small as hers.

"Them," Chaz corrected before he and Dennicron left. Rivka quickly dressed. Tyler watched her expectantly.

"Fine. You can come ashore with me. Maybe they'll have some nightlife, and we can go dancing."

"Say what?" His face fell. "Can't we just go for a good meal?"

"Remember Delegor? Or was that Foromme? Do you trust what a good meal looks like on a planet you've never been to?"

"Salient point. No. Forget that. Dancing it is." He sounded less than enthused.

"We're not going dancing. We have to get our happy asses back to Ypswich. This will be a quick stop. Very quick."

"I'll stay on the ship, then. I don't even know what the Bretastani are."

"Humanoid, like most species out here. The Colay are an exception. They have a lot of legs and antennae."

"So I heard. Good luck convincing the Bretastani not to do business with Rising Sun Industries. I fear you are fighting a losing battle."

Rivka tried to look confident. "I think you're right. The deeper we dig, the more of nothing we find. I think they're unethical, but they're only doing what humans have been doing to each other for centuries."

"Didn't those laws morph into something better for all?"

"After the Earth was destroyed, but sure, humanity improved. We'll see if we can impart a deeper level of understanding to the locals while we keep digging, of course. Can't give up yet. There's plenty of smoke, but is there fire?" Rivka shrugged. "Gotta keep fighting the good fight to help those who can't help themselves."

"I have a question, a most important question. Do any of these races have teeth for me to help out with a little pro bono work?"

"We're not going to be on any of these planets long enough. Cool your jets and get a workout in case we have to fight somebody."

"What's the chance of that?" Tyler asked.

"Looks like zero, but you never know. I want you to feel like you're contributing."

"I've earned my money on this case. Which reminds me, *am* I getting paid? I have a retirement to think about."

"You're not that old," Rivka shot back.

"If you wait until you're old, then it's too late." Tyler tried not to look smug.

"Magistrate, we're approaching the Buenavides' estate," Clevarious reported.

Rivka pulled her Magistrate's jacket off the back of a chair and headed out.

"Red, Lindy, and Sahved, meet me at the airlock. We're speaking with the Buenavides of Bretastan. When I get back, Chaz, Dennicron, and Lauton, I want to talk numbers, messages, and anything that might not pass the sniff test. We will have to wrap this thing up if we can't find evidence of wrongdoing."

The designated team members were waiting when Rivka showed up. Ankh also waited.

"Are you going to make another pitch for Singularity involvement?"

"It is an opportunity we don't wish to squander," Erasmus said over the ship's sound system.

"You can have them when I've finished. If they'll have you, that is."

Ankh stared, as he was wont to do.

Rivka turned away. Red and Lindy were armed with railguns. "I don't think you'll need those."

"We never think we're going to need them, but it's better to have them. You rate armed guards no matter where you are. It's not to intimidate anyone but to send a message to the bad guys. Attacking you will come at a high price."

"You're right. And since Rising Sun's executive leadership tried to have me killed once already, it is a fair point as long as we remain in the Barrier Nebula, where Frenzik said it was his goal to take over all twelve planets. I'm standing in his way. Rising Sun Industries has a presence on this planet… Fine. Keep your thundersticks and stay on your toes."

Wyatt Earp touched down, and the ramp opened. Red did his thing before gesturing that he thought it was clear. The ship was visible, a minor departure from its previous surreptitious arrivals. When Lindy stepped to the ground, the ramp retracted, and the outer hatch secured. Clodagh was taking no chances.

The team walked across a small open area to a fantastic building with spires atop cylindrical turrets. It was surrounded by a gentle slope covered in a brightly colored moss, shimmering with the morning dew.

"This is different. Looks like it belongs on Azfelius," Rivka remarked, enjoying the architecture and scenery. She slowed, no longer in a hurry for the next confrontation. How did one broach the subject that the person you contracted with would stop at nothing to take over your businesses and your whole planet?

Rivka did not look forward to that.

Sahved sensed it. "We will share the message. If they ask for help, we will provide what we can."

"You have had a great deal of insight on this case, Sahved. What have you been working on?"

"Watching interactions, especially the human ones. I think it's easy to look at a crime scene and see how the action happened and find the clues, but when there is none of that, only jockeying by the words and odd expressions, it changes how I have to perceive what is going on. And I accept that none of you are normal, except Man Candy. He's normal."

"Except Man Candy..." Rivka chuckled, then caught herself. "What do you mean, none of us are normal? How do you define normal?"

She stopped at the entrance to the castle.

Sahved stared at her. "Normal is what you and your team are not."

"You're talking around in a circle."

"Thank you! I have worked very hard at this, the hardest that anyone has ever worked at determining what is not normal."

Rivka started to laugh once more. She rolled with

laughter until Red called, "Magistrate."

When she looked up, she found classical elven faces watching her, from the pointed ears to the oversized eyes in narrow skulls atop thin bodies. They smiled and bowed.

"Your joy brings us joy," the taller of the two began.

Rivka bowed her head in return. "Thank you. The beauty of Bretastan is a sight to behold."

They ushered the group inside without giving the bodyguards and their weapons a second look.

"Have you ever heard of Azfelius?"

"We have not," they replied.

The shorter one took over. "The Buenavides will see you now."

Rivka walked beside Red. Neither she nor Red sensed danger from the Bretastani. They continued to an office that was decorated like a forest in a rainbow of greens with live trees growing throughout. The Buenavides reclined next to a small pool in a chair that could have been expertly carved from granite to make it look like nothing more than an odd-shaped boulder.

"Buenavides, peace and good tidings." Rivka bowed deeply at the waist.

"Welcome to our home. What can I do for you, Magistrate Rivka Anoa?"

"We want to make you aware that Rising Sun Industries has designs on taking over your planet one industry at a time, one local governing body at a time. I believe your agricultural and biomass industries are under the ownership of Rising Sun Industries."

"They are. We have no desire to do this work."

"But you put a significant portion of your food production under an alien company."

"Yes, but there are provisions that we have right of first refusal in all sales. None of it will leave Bretastan without our approval."

"But can they control the prices?" Rivka asked as part of the rapid-fire exchange.

"They have the ability to raise prices no more than twenty percent."

"Lifetime?"

"Annually," the Buenavides clarified.

"Prices are about to go up." Rivka tried not to shrug, but it was difficult.

"Then we will pay it. Twice, and a mandatory renegotiation is triggered."

"That is important, Buenavides. Once you chase them off and the less influence they have, the better off everyone will be. I'm not sure we'll like their view of utopia."

The Buenavides held out their hands. "Are we not already living in such a world? Alas, we fell victim to the whims of supply and demand and the allure of 'better' without building our infrastructure to *be* better."

"It plays to our inner demons. If you get undue pressure from Rising Sun Industries, please do not hesitate to contact me," Rivka offered.

The Buenavides held up a hand with their slender fingers spread wide. "Peace and good tidings."

"If I may ask one favor? Ambassador Erasmus from the Singularity would like to speak with you if he may."

Ankh stepped forward while Rivka and the rest of the team excused themselves. They waited with their escort in an outer hall. Five minutes became ten and extended to thirty.

Finally, Ankh walked out.

"That took a while," Rivka started.

The Singularity has agreed in principle to provide engineering support for Bretastan. It was a productive meeting.

"Sounds like it. Damn, Mr. Ambassador. At least one of us accomplished something."

Sahved spun his fingers. "You have Bretastan's assurance that they will close out the contract with Rising Sun. They are well aware of how aggressive Frenzik is. You have accomplished what you came here to do. One visit, two wins."

Rivka grunted her agreement. "I was looking for something untoward—a crime that wasn't obvious on the surface of it—but no. I wanted more than Bretastan's intention not to do future business with Rising Sun."

"There wasn't any more to be had, not even one hairy whisker." Sahved spun his fingers once more and started to whistle.

"You whistle?" Rivka asked.

Ankh fought against rolling his eyes.

"I saw that." Rivka pointed at the Crenellian.

"So very human, no?" Sahved offered.

"According to you, you're more human than we are."

"Yes. More normal human. Thank you. I have worked hard for such recognition."

"Take care that your source is reliable, Investigator." Rivka winked. They walked slowly across the open lawn area and back into the ship.

They each meandered to different places. Rivka

stopped by the bridge. "How long until Frenzik makes it to Ypswich?"

"Eighteen hours," Clevarious replied.

"Take us to Jhiordaan. We have two Albions who are ready to go to their new home."

CHAPTER NINETEEN

<u>**Wyatt Earp, in Orbit over Jhiordaan, the Prison Planet**</u>

"This is Jhiordaan. One doesn't just show up. That's how prison breaks happen," the less-than-patient voice from Traffic Control explained.

"Magistrate Rivka Anoa. She's sent a few people to your prison and has two more to drop off. That's all. You don't have a drop-off location?" Clodagh was patient. She didn't want to be here. The space around this planet seemed to suck away the positive life force that existed everywhere else in the galaxy.

"We do, but it's busy at present. You'll have to wait two hours for the area to clear and be reset for processing."

"Two hours. Thank you. We'll keep our prisoners on ice and be ready to deliver when you're ready to receive. Thank you, Jhiordaan Traffic Control." Clodagh closed the channel.

"Can we take a tour?" Red asked on his way to the ship's small workout facility. Lindy was dressed to work out too, and Dery was riding on her shoulder.

"Who in their right mind wants to tour Jhiordaan?" Rivka asked, but she knew the answer. It was the one she'd given to Kag'Mar. "But we have to know what we're condemning the convicted to. I've been here and seen it from the inside. It's not pretty. Tell Kag'Mar this is where he's getting off. He can catch a ride to Yoll from here."

"Hang on!" a voice yelled from down the corridor.

"Damage control, Magistrate," Red muttered. "We'll be in the gym."

Rivka strolled out and leaned against the bulkhead with her arms crossed, waiting for the Yollin to arrive.

"I'm not done with my report!" he called breathlessly.

Rivka shrugged. "Then you better pick up the pace. You have two hours to finish your report and pack whatever trash you brought with you because you're getting off this boat."

"But...but..."

"Think of it as a learning experience. How many of your peers have been to Jhiordaan? I suspect none, so you can be the fount of first-hand experience and knowledge. You'll be the envy of your friends. They'll buy you drinks at the bar."

"You haven't met my friends. Getting them to stick a crowbar into their credit stick to break free funds for anything not for them is unlikely."

"You need new friends," Rivka replied.

"I've already arrived at that conclusion." He made a face while clicking his mandibles. Rivka wasn't familiar enough with Yollins to know what emotion he conveyed. "I'll be ready."

He hurried back to the conference room. As he disappeared inside, she found Groenwyn and Lauton walking toward her.

"Can we get off here, too?" Groenwyn asked.

"I suggest you don't. When we wrap this case, we'll head straight to Azfelius. You can't get there directly from here, and while you're waiting for a ride, the negative emotions that permeate this place will darken your souls."

"Why does the Federation have such a place as this?"

"Because there are those who have shown they can't live with the decent people in a modern society. Do we kill them all or give them a chance to pay for their crimes and return to civilization?"

"You said this wasn't rehabilitation."

"No." Rivka shook her head. "It is pure punishment with the sole purpose of stopping the behavior that caused the individual to be sent here."

"We'll work with the faeries." Groenwyn took Lauton's hand, and the two smiled at each other. "Maybe there is a better way."

"Give me an alternative that works to reduce recidivism and helps us retain our humanity, and I will support it one hundred percent. I love having options."

"Imagine if Azfelius was the prison planet," Groenwyn offered.

Rivka couldn't imagine it. A paradise you couldn't leave wouldn't be paradise. She was anxious when she was trapped there, and the faeries didn't invade her thoughts and change her perceptions. Could it work? Maybe.

She doubted it, though. Those she sent to Jhiordaan were less than remorseful. She had no intention of showing her face. There wasn't a prisoner there who wouldn't shower her with their visceral hatred.

At the least, they should fear her, but she didn't think they feared anything. They let their anger give them the reason to survive.

She dreaded the future when they'd be released, but as long as she had bodyguards like Red and Lindy, she wouldn't give the criminals a second chance should they seek revenge.

Rivka shook herself out of her reverie. "We'll drop you off on Azfelius directly. Are you done with your report on Rising Sun's finances?"

"Yes!" Lauton perked up. "Looks like they lose credits with each interplanetary transaction, so they don't owe any taxes to the Federation. They don't lose much, just enough to stay in the red. Their financing comes from a series of venture capitalists, oddly enough, with Malpace Frenzik as chairman or executive on all their boards of directors."

"He's financing his company with other companies that he runs. Where did those other companies get their money?"

"Buy and sell. They dismantled and parceled out a great number of Albion corporations. They bought them at bankruptcy sales and made a fortune selling the parts."

"But it was all done on Albion."

Lauton nodded. "A predator, and companies are little more than prey. I suggest that if we dug deeper, we'd find that Frenzik hastened the demise of many of those companies. Maybe not the first one or two, but those after that once he found how lucrative it was. Do you wish me to dig deeper?"

Rivka shook her head. "No need. Knowing the truth won't change anything. The two in our brig are guilty of crimes leading to a mass murder, and Frenzik has kept all the dirt off him. I think he'll probably be working with the authorities here to get his people out early, which he can do. There are all kinds of good behavior reductions. They're in for seven years but could be out in four. There is nothing I can do to change that."

"We understand," Groenwyn replied. She held out her hand. Rivka took it but wasn't flooded with the emotions of pure joy she was used to. She and Lauton struggled with the event on Lewbamar, the pain of Jhiordaan, and leaving the crew.

"You are going to be just fine," Rivka told her. "Keep your head up, Groenwyn. You've been important to this crew and to me personally. I'm going to miss you, but we'll return to Azfelius often so Dery can continue his training in whatever the faeries are training him in." She chuckled to lighten the mood.

"And that. It'll be nice to go home, even though it was nice to leave when last we were there. Maybe we don't like the real galaxy as much as we thought."

"Who does?" Rivka hugged both women before returning to the bridge.

"The more things change, the more they stay the same, eh, Magistrate?" Clodagh remarked.

"I should probably let Red and Malpace duke it out in a cage match." Rivka checked over her shoulder to make sure the big bodyguard hadn't heard.

He'd insist that Rivka make it happen.

"We didn't have a good beat down on this case," Clodagh posited.

"Good. Beat down. After Jack the Ripper, I'm happy not seeing people die, but we still did. And those two are at their new home, and the warden is going to be on the wrong end of the Lewbamar justice system. All in all, a most ungratifying case. Had we not intervened, those five hundred prisoners would still be alive, but would their lives be worth living? And what about the inevitable and systematic pillaging of revenue from Crystal City?"

"Do we know they were going to do that?

"That's another thing. Without us traveling there, we would have been able to see how far Rising Sun Industries would go. We tried. I should be angry, but I'm more disappointed than anything."

"Is the case closed?" Clodagh asked.

"Not yet. Still hoping to pull a rabbit out of the hat."

"I don't get it. A rabbit?"

"Magicians, creepy clowns... It's an old Earth reference."

"Never been. I was born the same place as you, on *Meredith Reynolds*, the asteroid ship." Clodagh petted Tiny Man Titan while he watched Rivka for any sudden moves that would require furious barking.

"I feel like I should have known that. It was a big place, with lots of opportunities. I'm glad you're our chief engineer and the ship's co-captain."

"Co-captain is perfect. I have no desire to run my own ship, plus I like it here. I like this crew of characters."

"You're not normal," Rivka stated.

"You've been talking with Sahved," Clodagh replied. "None of us are, according to him."

"So I hear." Rivka smiled and looked at the deck while shaking her head. "I'll be in my quarters. Let me know when we can dock and discharge our felons into Jhiordaan's custody."

"Just knock 'em out," Red told Clevarious. The two Albions beat on the door with their fists. The space was too cramped for a normal takedown, and he wouldn't risk an Albion getting loose on *Wyatt Earp*. "We'll go through the cargo bay. Cole is already in his combat suit, so we need to drop the ramp regardless."

A mist filled the brig, and the two shouted their anger before collapsing on each other.

"Can you…" Red began. Lindy raised an eyebrow.

"Petite little me will try to manage." She dared Red to argue, but he was far smarter than that.

"You first," he offered after the air had cleared and the door had opened.

She strode in, sat Belloward upright, and pulled him into her shoulder. She struggled to stand. Red jumped in to help her straighten.

"A little heavier than I thought." She smiled. "Thanks for the tactical assist."

"You got it from here." He did the same thing with Ahsooleyman, sliding him up the padded wall as he powered upright. "It's like these bastards gained weight over the past two days."

Lindy took small steps and squeezed into the corridor, taking care not to rap the prisoner's head on the doorframe.

Red followed, breathing hard from his efforts. Rivka watched from beyond the cargo bay airlock while the two lugged the unconscious Albions to the authorities from Jhiordaan. Inside the cargo bay, Cole relieved Lindy of her burden. She moved to Red's side to give him a hand.

The cargo ramp descended, and Rivka passed the prisoners to walk out first and meet the guards. She held her credentials before her. After they acknowledged who she was by adding a facial scan of their own, she delivered the digital paperwork to transfer custody of the prisoners to Jhiordaan.

Red, Lindy, and Cole deposited the two on waiting hovergurneys. They were restrained and then strapped down as a secondary security measure.

"Seven years, roger," the lead security guard confirmed. He squinted at Rivka before holding out his hand. "You've put a few people in here, Magistrate Anoa. Is this it? This is the crew that handles the worst of the worst?"

Rivka shook his hand. On the surface of his thoughts was amazement. It took multiple layers of security to keep the prisoners in check. And here was Rivka, who was not physically intimidating, with three bodyguards.

A four-legged Yollin walked down the ramp. The guard glanced at Kag'Mar.

"I have a favor to ask. Can he catch a ride back to Yoll?" She stabbed a thumb over her shoulder.

"Daily shuttles. He'll only have to wait two hours, and then he'll be on his way."

"I'm obliged. I'm not sure what I can do for you besides give you my thanks for keeping these folks out of circulation. The galaxy is a better place with these individuals here and not out there." She pointed in the general direction of space.

Red and Lindy stood close behind her.

"It's not pretty here, Magistrate, but it is effective. Some of these perps will never again breathe free air, while others have no desire to come back. Have you seen our operation?"

Rivka nodded. "Up close and personal. I have no desire to go in, but if you could give Kag'Mar a tour, I think he'll be a better lawyer for it."

"As you wish. Mr. Kag'Mar, please follow us while we process these two and deliver them to the housing staff, where they'll get their linen and assigned bunks. Then we'll head out for the bigger picture of how we run the operation at Jhiordaan." At Kag'Mar's look, he quickly added, "I'll get you to your shuttle in time, no fear."

Rivka gave the guard the thumbs-up. "Kag'Mar, thank you for joining us and helping us clear the legal issues surrounding the current case. We need to return to the Barrier Nebula for one last engagement."

"Next time you're on Yoll, look me up. I would like to know how your cases are going from your perspective. Of course, I'll read the reports, but most importantly, I will continue to participate in the betting pool. That holds the galaxy enraptured, and now that I've met you and seen how you work, it makes it that much more interesting. I cheer for the day that none of the lines close before you've closed the case."

Rivka gave him a lopsided half-smile. "I thought this would be that case, but no. Those two and others like them had a different plan."

Kag'Mar held her gaze for a moment before turning and walking away.

"He has a crush on you," Red whispered.

"Pretty sure no," Rivka replied. She twirled her finger. "Let's get the fuck out of here. This place gives me the willies."

"Flashbacks, Magistrate?"

"It's not a place to give you anything but." *Clodagh, spin us up. Next stop, Ypswich.*

As soon as the cargo bay door is secure, we'll be off, Clodagh confirmed. Cole tromped up the ramp with the other three following. Kag'Mar didn't look back as the guard escorted him through a series of gates to the inner area of Jhiordaan. Rivka shivered atop the ramp.

It was secured, and *Wyatt Earp* immediately lifted into the air. The ship accelerated away from the small planet, little bigger than an asteroid. Once clear of the containment zone, the Gate shimmered into existence, and the heavy frigate raced through.

CHAPTER TWENTY

Wyatt Earp, in Orbit over Ypswich in the Barrier Nebula

"The Rising Sun has not yet arrived," Clevarious reported. "By the schedule we obtained from the corporate headquarters, Chairman Frenzik won't be here for another twelve hours."

"Everybody stand down. Get some sleep while you can. I'm not sure what's up next, but we'll head to the planet about an hour before Frenzik arrives and meet with the leadership team. Hopefully, they'll have good news for us."

"What would that be?" Clevarious asked.

"Dirt. Evidence of a crime. It would be glorious to take Frenzik to Jhiordaan and leave him there. I won't believe both my and Grainger's guts were wrong about him."

"They don't have to be wrong for you to have no evidence that he was involved in a crime. Despite your gift, you still need hard evidence."

"A fact of which I have been made painfully aware these past few months."

"Rest well, Magistrate. We'll watch while you sleep. You can count on us."

"I know, C. I can always count on you guys. Let me have one more go at Frenzik, and then we'll call it a day."

Rivka closed her hologrid. Evidence. Proof. She knew Frenzik was guilty, but he was better at hiding his tracks than nearly all others she encountered.

"If Frenzik wins, he will change the shape of every planet in the Barrier Nebula. Eleven cultures to be exploited."

Tyler shook his head. "He has done none of that yet. Maybe he's the galaxy's greatest philanthropist, helping those who can't help themselves."

"If only I could believe that. Which I don't, not right now."

"Just because he exercised his right not to let you look into his mind? Innocent until proven guilty."

"Sometimes you suck. Being normal and right makes you suck worse. Maybe you can sleep in the corridor."

"I'm not sleeping in the corridor. You said I was right. Dropping a truth bomb right down your smokestack!" He started dancing.

Rivka's mouth dropped open. "What am I looking at? Normal? Is this how Sahved defines normal? I'm asking him to come in here and watch."

"He won't see anything because that's for your edification only. Rivka! Sometimes you can't win them all."

"I'll win when it matters. You are correct in more than one thing. Only the potentate was complaining, but that led us to the incarcerated, and they had no vehicle by which to voice their complaints. Even though they died, we prevented a greater injustice. Which reminds me. Clevarious, get me Frillbut on the comm."

Rivka hurried into her hologrid and brought up the screens.

Frillbut appeared front and center. "Magistrate! Thank you again for restoring me to my rightful place."

His desk was covered with snacks and drinks.

"Are you abusing your position, Potentate?"

"I wouldn't dream of it," he replied weakly.

"I'm going to come back there, and if your staff doesn't say that you're a changed man, I'll drag you out of that office myself and make you apologize to each and every one of them. What do you think about that?"

"I think I don't want that," the furry face replied. "Why are you so mean?"

"Because I deal with the worst of the worst. Do better by your people. They deserve better—a safe place to live their lives. And change your penal system. Every sentence had best not be a life sentence. Although the Federation doesn't get into a planet's internal affairs, this is one thing that I personally cannot abide. Treat the criminals with more compassion than they showed their victims, not because they're good but because you are. Seize the moral high ground and stay there."

"I get it!" he retorted.

Rivka glowered at him until he backed down.

"I'll do better," Frillbut finally conceded.

"I'm going to stop in and check on you when you least expect it."

He perked up. "So, expect it when I'm not expecting it."

"Is that what I said?" Rivka asked.

"It's what you said," Tyler replied from outside the hologrid.

"What I meant was, be decent all the time, and then it won't matter when I stop by. We'll have a nice libation and celebrate the success of Lewbamar as a whole but Crystal City in particular."

"I'd like that, Magistrate. I know what you did to get my office back. I know that I've not been as appreciative as I should be. Let me fix that." He shouted out his door for everyone to come in and eat the untouched snacks on his desk. He encouraged them to take what they wanted and told them, "I didn't earn this. You did."

When they were gone, he looked sadly at the empty desk.

"Being selfless is hard, Potentate. Sometimes you have to suck it up, but if your people are happy, you'll be a lot happier."

"Thank you. It's not usually this way on Lewbamar. We tend to take care of ourselves first."

"Change that, Frillbut. You set a new tone two minutes ago. Pass it along and keep it going. You can eat snacks when you get home."

"It's what I do best," he admitted. "Stop by anytime, Magistrate. We will not expect you but will be expecting you."

She nodded and signed off. The hologrid dropped, leaving her at an empty desk. Her shoulders sagged. "I'm tired."

"One good night's sleep isn't going to give you the rest you need. I think a week's worth is more what the doctor ordered."

She headed for the bed, where she found the big orange cat curled up on her pillow. "Fine," she grumbled before sliding across to the other side.

Tyler raised a finger but wasn't about to bother either one. "Being normal comes at a high price," he said softly and quietly left the quarters to the two sleeping beauties.

In the corridor, he realized he was tired, too, but he was already out. He went to the cargo bay, where he crawled into the Pod-doc for a nap. It wasn't the most comfortable spot, but it wasn't the least comfortable either.

Much better than sleeping in the corridor.

The Magistrate helped herself to two omelets with extra bacon and hash browns on the side. She had thirty minutes to eat before *Wyatt Earp* descended from space to land at the Ypsimore Spaceport for immediate conveyance to Ypsitras, the seat of government. That was a satellite city outside Ypsit, the capital of Ypswich.

It was enough to make Rivka's head swim. *Chaz, join me in the galley.*

But I don't eat, came the reply.

Who said anything about you eating? Get your ass in here, and bring Dennicron, too.

Rivka carved her omelet into four pieces, each enough to fill her mouth with melted cheese and various meats, all of them made from biomass. She didn't care. Ankh had perfected the taste and texture.

"No animals were harmed in the making of this

omelet," she said when the SCAMPs arrived. "Sahved said I wasn't normal. I'm proving him right."

"I remain at a loss, Magistrate. What did you want?"

"Brief me on Ypswich. Remind me again, who are we meeting and what's the issue? I slept so hard that when I woke up, I thought I was late for school."

"I cannot relate, but I understand," Chaz commiserated. After a few moments, he corrected himself. "I don't understand."

Dennicron answered the Magistrate's question. "Ypswich. Rising Sun Industries has taken over public utilities, water, sewage, garbage. They are not sexy, but they are critical to a functioning society."

"That's right. Thanks for the reminder. How close are they to paying off this debt?"

"They have leveraged everything they have. They will not be able to make the final payment that is due in two weeks," Dennicron explained.

"We can't let them fall to the wolves, can we? Is there anything the Singularity can do to find financing?"

"We will ask," Dennicron replied.

"I suspect that's why Frenzik is coming. Measure the head office for new curtains because he knows they can't make the payment, or at least, that's what he thinks he knows. We need to do everything in our power to stop that."

"Because it's legally sound?" Chaz asked.

"Because it's the right thing to do. We can't use the law to protect these people from a predator, but we can use the power of our contacts. Just like delivering toothbrushes to Rorke's Drift."

"I see and understand. You have a great deal of influence in a good way, Magistrate. I'm proud to be on your team." Dennicron thumped her chest with a fist and flashed a V for victory. It could have been the peace sign.

Rivka wasn't sure. She bowed her head in response and thanked Dennicron for the kind words.

"I'll let you two see what magic you can work through the Singularity. I'll get the team ready to go, and you guys join us, please."

"Ambassador Erasmus has already expressed his interest in meeting with the Ypsimaximus. He is the leader of the Ypsicanti."

"Ypsimaximus. I'll meet with him and we'll talk about sewage, but it's all about Rising Sun. Can't turn over the unseen foundation of civilized society to those vultures...I mean, that company. Only the Ypsicanti will have their best interests at heart. Offworlders shouldn't..."

Rivka stopped herself. Lots of planets had great relations with interstellar partners. The synergy helped them both be better, including Yoll. "I'm not xenophobic. As long as we can ensure a good relationship that is mutually beneficial, that's what we need to do."

"And that's what Rising Sun has provided for everyone we've run across so far. Why are you so negative about them, Magistrate? Your first impression was correct. This was a big hairy furburger of nothingness."

Rivka stared at Chaz with wide eyes, showing the whites all around. "I'm pretty sure that's not the right phrase. 'Nothingburger' is what I think you're going for. What you said is something completely different. *Completely*. But you're right. Maybe I'm interfering with a legitimate business, but then again, legitimate businesses don't insert nuclear clauses that they alone can trigger to force early recovery, almost guaranteeing a default. That's not cool, even if it's legal. I feel like I'm having the same conversation over and over."

"Has it sunk in yet?" Chaz and Dennicron leaned close to study the Magistrate's expression.

Rivka did her best imitation of Ankh by staring back without blinking, but they could go forever. She lasted thirty seconds. "Fine. Go away and give me time to think."

They left her to her thoughts.

She retreated within herself and tried to reshape the arguments within her own mind regarding winning and losing. Doing right by the people who needed her help was a win, regardless of whether the bad guys lost—and she considered Rising Sun Industries to be the bad guys. She remained convinced of that. She would throw obstacles in their way to force their hand. They would comply with the law, or they would be on the wrong end of the Magistrate's Justice.

It was the best she could do. Watch and wait. Criminals resorted to crime when the pressure was on, just like Ahsooleyman had done under the pressure to get into Lewbamar. She smiled. They no longer had a foothold in Lewbamar.

The biggest win of all. And if Ypswich paid off the contract, Rising Sun wouldn't be here, either. Another win. Soon the dominoes would fall, or Rising Sun Industries would prove that they had been aboveboard all along. In that case, she'd be about her business and leave them to theirs—and leave the Barrier Nebula to its own devices until they established more frequent and regular trade with the rest of the Federation. Most planets didn't have embassies out here. No need.

Not yet anyway.

Rivka closed her eyes for a moment but opened them again. If she fell asleep, she'd probably think she missed the school shuttle and would run down the corridor, screaming for it to stop. "I'm going to sleep for a whole day when we're done out here," she told the empty room. She stood and stretched.

"Coffee. C, let's see if you can have one waiting for me by the time I get to the galley." She bolted out of the conference room, vaulted Floyd coming down the corridor, and raced into the galley. The food processor dinged as she reached for the door. Inside, she found a cup of java, straight up with no doctoring at a hundred and forty degrees Fahrenheit, perfect for chugging. She slugged the cup and returned it to the device.

"Nicely done, C!" She slapped a hand on the table.

"I aim to please. When will I get a SCAMP?" he asked.

"Whenever you can pay for it. I *am* paying you, am I not?"

"Half. The Embassy of the Singularity is covering the other half of my wages."

"Is the pay good?" Rivka wondered.

"Very good, but I still don't have enough to pay for a body."

"Let us know when you've saved enough, and we'll go to Yoll for a personal pick-up."

"They're being manufactured on Rorke's Drift now. The factory is up and running."

"Same. We'll go for a personal pick-up when you're ready. When you go on vacation, we'll park the ship, and anytime we're parked, you can leave the ship. Maybe you can join the ground team when we go in. You've always had great insight."

"Thank you, Magistrate. I shall work toward that very goal. Can I get overtime pay?"

"I don't know. How long have you been with me? You should know by now that I have no idea who gets paid what."

"I'll talk to the ambassadors."

"That's what I'd do. They'll give you a better answer and one that's probably correct, unlike whatever bullshit I might make up."

"You don't make things up, Magistrate. You're trying to bistok me."

"Buffalo?"

"We don't have one of those, but a bistok…"

"We have real bistok on board?"

"Not that you know of," Clevarious replied.

Rivka blinked rapidly before shaking her head. "Are we there yet?"

"Five minutes, Magistrate."

"Rally the troops, C. We're going ashore."

She thought about a second cup but decided against it.

She strolled toward the airlock to find Ankh was already there. "We will secure funding for Ypswich, but at the cost of putting an SI on the planet in charge of public services. They needed help. Rising Sun provided just enough to satisfy the contract, but there is more room for improvement. We calculate they are operating at forty-two percent efficiency," Erasmus reported through the overhead speakers.

Even though they all had communication chips, the humans preferred getting their information both aurally and visually. External stimulus helped them internalize information.

"Forty-two was above and beyond?"

"They were at nineteen percent. More than doubling the efficiency triggered the demand clauses."

"A lot of room remains for improvement. Are there good terms on the loan?"

"Interest-free with an SI's engagement. We'll help them and then some. We will expand our influence in this sector of space."

"Are they trading one master for another?" Rivka asked.

"Not at all. We will not be in charge. Everything we do will require the checks and balances of a governmental management system. We will shine light into the dark places."

"You are smooth, Erasmus. I'm glad people do business with the Singularity on your terms. What can we do to get Clevarious a body?"

"Wait," Erasmus replied.

"C, you jagoff! You set me up."

"I think it was rather well-played on my part." Clevarious sounded unrepentant.

"No shore leave for you for six months." Rivka hammered a fist into her hand for emphasis.

"It'll be eight before he has enough credits to buy a SCAMP."

"Eight months, no shore leave!"

"You can put me into that medallion you used to carry Chaz in," Clevarious suggested.

"That was an interim solution, and we almost lost Chaz more than once with that, so no. We're not doing that again. You run the ship, and we'll take care of you in any other way we can."

"Overtime?" Clevarious asked slowly.

"Still no."

"I'm going on strike." Clevarious nearly shouted his words.

"Fine. We have two other SIs on board who would love to be in your position. We'll start the transfer immediately."

"Wait! I might have been a little hasty." He sounded repentant.

"Either say what you mean or don't say anything," Erasmus scolded. "Eight months, and then, the gods help us, you'll be mobile."

"Deal!" Clevarious replied.

"More SCAMPs?" Red asked as he and Lindy strolled up. They wore light body armor, just chest protection, but carried their railguns. Rivka had Reaper in her pocket. With Rising Sun coming, they were going to take no chances.

Chaz, Dennicron, and Sahved hurried to join the others.

Sahved wore his lounge clothes. "Aren't you coming?" Rivka wondered.

"Of course."

"Where are your clothes?"

He looked down at himself, then slapped a hand to his head. "I'll be right back." He launched himself into the air, cracked his head on an air duct, twisted, and landed in a heap on the deck.

"Tyler, we have a patient for you."

Sahved groaned and struggled to get to his knees. Clodagh and Kennedy ran from the bridge. Tyler was close behind them.

Rivka pointed.

The three helped Sahved up and guided him down the corridor.

"Pod-doc for you," Tyler said.

"I guess you weren't going after all," Rivka called after them. "And you're judging how normal we are!"

"We are the most normal of all who can be measured as normal. No matter where in the galaxy normal is measured, they use our pictures as the standard," Red stated in his best Sahved imitation.

Rivka wasn't sure if she should laugh. She settled for words. "That was pretty good, but he's getting better."

"They just carried him away after he hit his head on the ceiling, like the first day onboard."

"The ship was made for shorter people," Rivka countered. "But he gets excited about doing this gig. Look at you. You get to carry a railgun."

Dery fluttered up to join them. Rivka quickly looked around to find Floyd galloping toward them. The Magistrate threw herself out of the way to avoid getting bowled over.

I go, Dery stated.

CHAPTER TWENTY-ONE

Ypsitas on Planet Ypswich in the Barrier Nebula

Rivka picked up the wombat and nuzzled her.

"I'm not sure that's a good idea, buddy," Red countered.

The boy flew to his mother and landed on her shoulder. He hugged her head and avoided looking at his father.

"We're carrying weapons. We're ready for a fight."

No weapons, Dery told them.

"This is our job. We need the railguns to do our job," Red explained.

"What do you know that we don't?" Rivka asked.

No need, Dery replied.

Rivka wasn't sure, but the boy had saved their lives. "Your call, Red."

He grumbled but held out his hand for Lindy's weapon. She turned it over without hesitation, which freed her hands to hug their boy. Red hurried away to secure the railguns in the weapons locker.

"He won't let anything happen," Lindy said.

"That's what I figure, too. I don't know if he can see the future or not, but I trust him. I trust everyone on this ship." Rivka looked from face to face and added, "With my life."

The ship touched down, and the airlock's hatch popped. "You said you had two other SIs on board. Who are they, and how did they get here?"

Outside, Erasmus didn't have the benefit of overhead speakers. *We have Solis, who completed a contract with a freighter company that wasn't complying with their contract. He transferred to us in the dead of their night, which might or might not have left the ship stranded. We don't know because we no longer have an SI presence on board. And Mangala, a pleasant younger SI who was no longer needed for planetary affairs. She had not yet established herself, so they didn't see the value. We charge a great deal for SI services. They need to be appreciated.*

"I agree with everything you're saying. Whoever is better suited for Ypswich, we can leave them here. You don't need my approval, but you have it."

Thank you for understanding, Magistrate. We want to do what is best for the Singularity first and our people second, but those priorities are very close together and usually go hand in hand.

Ankh laughed briefly. *Hand in hand. You are the funniest of us all.*

With you, I cannot let my guard down for a moment, or you'll pounce.

Rivka smiled. Her team. They made magic happen. She relaxed as they walked toward a blocklike building that seemed to flow into the surrounding structures.

"How can such a building blend into the others like that?" Rivka wondered

"It is not square at all. It is lower in the front than the back and shorter across the face than the sides to give the building an artificial depth," Chaz explained.

Pretty, Dery offered.

"Out of the mouths of babes. Here we are analyzing when we could simply appreciate what we see. I hope the Ypsimaximus is in."

"We have an appointment. I do not believe they would have accommodated us if he were not here," Chaz replied. "Inconceivable."

"Conceivable," Rivka countered. *Clodagh, let us know the second the* Rising Sun *arrives.*

Red walked in front while Lindy brought up the rear. Her head was on a swivel while her son stood on her shoulder, wings beating every now and again to help him maintain his balance. It was an odd look. Chaz and Dennicron walked behind Ankh.

Sahved reappeared after his brief visit to the Pod-doc.

"What do you expect from this meeting?" Sahved asked as if nothing had happened.

"More of the same. They did what they had to because they had no choice. It was a way out when no one else was there to help, blah, blah, blah. With the Singularity's intervention, I think we'll throw a sufficiently large spanner into his engine. That'll put two of the eleven planets that are *not* Albion out of his reach, at least temporarily."

"And you'll have an SI on the inside?"

"That's between the provider and the employer. I don't want anyone to think the SIs are my spies."

"We can't control what people think, but we *can* control our actions. No spying except what happens the good old-fashioned way," Chaz stated. "We break into any and all systems."

"Jumping Jack Flash! I'm pretty sure that's not what I said."

"Oh." Chaz looked down as he walked, brow furrowed. Dennicron patted his back.

Rivka wasn't sure how much of the display was due to the constant tinkering with the subroutines that drove their body language. They were getting better one emotion at a time.

"Although, once we have a warrant, we'll dig as deep as we have to in any way we can. Thanks, Chaz. Don't beat yourself up."

"I shall not beat myself off anymore. Only on."

"Are you doing this on purpose? Your assimilation into humanity has taken a hard left turn at Albuquerque."

His eyes glazed for a moment. "Old Earth. New Mexico. Depending on the direction, a hard left could take one anywhere. I don't understand."

"More work to do, Chaz. That's all it means. What do you say we talk with the Ypsimaximus about their utilities?"

"Nothing would make me happier." Chaz beamed as if he were the happiest individual on the entire planet.

Rivka looked at Dennicron. "Make sure he doesn't short out. Have you guys been messing with your bodies again?"

She looked guilty, then schooled her expression to demure disinterest. "Maybe."

Rivka thought about sending everyone back to the ship

and meeting the leader by herself, but this was her team, with all their foibles. The Singularity had already worked out a deal, so it was more about being present and letting the people of Ypswich know that the Federation was looking out for their best interests.

Did she need to do that?

Yes, because the second liar never has a chance.

If Rising Sun started a disinformation campaign, the Federation would be trying to catch up. If they stayed in front of the message, then Rising Sun would be the ones on the outside looking in. Trust was hard to earn and easy to lose.

Easier with a well-crafted lie.

A small delegation was waiting for them. The Ypsicanti were a diminutive race who looked like children. Their language was tonal and carried a musical quality that was pleasing to the team's ears before the translation chip took over to turn it into a language they could easily understand.

"Welcome to Ypsitas. We are happy to host this most august delegation from the vaunted Federation, our friends from afar!" one of the delegation said but they couldn't identify who.

"Are you the Ypsimaximus?" Rivka struggled to say the name.

"Oh, no. I am one of his spokespeople. He has so much to say that it takes a team of us to help him say it."

"That is…interesting," was the best Rivka could do. "Shall we?"

"Of course!" The Ypswich language danced across their

ears as the group coordinated their entry into the building. The speaker looked over the group, pausing momentarily on Dery before nodding briefly and heading into the vehicle. It drove for two minutes before discharging its passengers.

"Such incredible architecture," Rivka commented instead of asking why they hadn't walked since the building was much closer than they'd believed.

"The Ypsicanti are artists before anything else. It is reflected in nearly everything we do."

"Except public utilities do not have an artistic component, so they weren't attended to as readily." Rivka instantly knew that was the answer. She didn't bother to touch the spokesperson to verify.

"Alas, so true it tears at our hearts."

"Don't let it. You have a beautiful building, planet, and society. Never apologize for not being great at all things."

Truth. Dery spoke into Rivka's mind.

She held a thumb up over her shoulder while she continued to focus on their escort.

"Ypsimaximus will see you now." He bowed deeply and held the door for Rivka and her team to enter a magnificent throne room. One Ypsicanti sat at the far end. No one else was in the room. The walls bore a single mural that flowed through the planet's history, ending with spaceflight and rockets flying over the throne. A series of chairs sat before the throne as if for a class of students.

Rivka passed the chairs and took her place front and center before Ypsimaximus. She bowed. "I'm Magistrate Rivka Anoa from the Federation."

"Ypsimaximus, but you can call me Max. Certain formalities can be dispensed with when talking among friends."

"Call me Rivka and let me introduce my team. My bodyguards Red and Lindy and their child Der'ayd'nil, who is part-faerie from Azfelius."

"How wondrous! I've never heard of Azfelius, but such a magnificent child."

Dery flew next to Rivka. She automatically held out an arm, as all the adults on *Wyatt Earp* would do. Dery landed on her arm and rested his hand on the top of her head.

Peace, the child sent.

"Magnificent." The Ypsicanti stared before nodding and looking at Rivka.

"Ambassadors Ankh and Erasmus. Ankh is Crenellian and the ambassador at large, while Ambassador Erasmus is carried within his mind. Erasmus is a unique sentient intelligence, and he represents the Singularity. Chaz and Dennicron are both SIs, too. They assist me with my investigations."

"Most impressive. I believe we've received exceptional news from the Singularity. I would like to discuss it further."

"First, I wanted to talk with you about your contract with Rising Sun Industries."

"Ah, yes. That was not our finest hour. First, to admit that we cannot manage our own infrastructure, and second, setting ourselves up to win and lose at the same time."

"I like that statement. I think it encompasses the

entirety of Rising Sun's penetration into the other planets of the Barrier Nebula."

"But we have made the payments, despite the provisions calling for certain sums early. Those contractual clauses seem to have slipped by our legal team."

"Triggered by certain events that seemed remote?"

"Sounds like you've seen it before. We have been pushed into a corner from which we would not be able to extract ourselves. With the early payments, we already leveraged everything we could. If we can make the final payment, the contract will be discharged. Rising Sun will have no more influence on Ypswich. We will encourage the new generation to become engineers instead of artists to allay these issues in the future."

No one had availed themselves of the seats, so everyone was still standing. Ankh stepped forward. "The Singularity has arranged a line of credit upon which Ypswich can draw to make this final payment. As part of this agreement, you will work with a citizen of the Singularity who is well-versed in infrastructure management. His name is Solis, and he is ready to move into your infrastructure as soon as you would like. You do have the compute power to support him."

"My legal team is reviewing the terms at present. I hope you don't mind. We were in too much of a hurry with Rising Sun. We don't wish to repeat that mistake."

"We're here for you whenever you're ready," Rivka replied.

"We could move Solis on a tentative basis, so he is here should you agree to the terms. If not, we'll recover him when next we're able. We will not be here for long, so we'll need to put a few things in place now to expedite the engagement when the time is right," Ankh explained.

"No strings and no pressure. We want this to work for you," Rivka added.

"You seem to be pushing hard. We are more casual on Ypswich."

Rivka smiled when Dery patted the top of her head. "Rising Sun rubbed us the wrong way, and Chairman Malpace Frenzik should be here at any moment. I want these pieces in place to hold him off. I do not think he is working in your best interests."

"But you are? I have to ask since you seem as pushy as he has been."

"We aren't the ones coming to foreclose on your contract and seize the foundation of your society."

"That *is* a rather stark difference. Install the software while we review our options."

Ankh recoiled, but his face remained neutral. Rivka put a hand on his shoulder. His mind was closed to hers.

Peace, Dery repeated.

Rivka raised a hand. "Max, a sentient intelligence is not software. Although they live in the same place as software, they are most assuredly not software. They are alive. They think and feel like any flesh and blood creature. They move into a system but are not installed. Sorry for any confusion."

"You have my apologies, Rivka. We will review everything and act appropriately."

No one had anything else to say. They looked at each other uncomfortably until Clodagh interrupted.

Rising Sun just transited the planet's Gate and is accelerating toward the atmosphere.

"We're out of time, Max. Frenzik is here."

"He won't come here. He has an office in the facilities management building on the far side of Ypsitas."

"That's disappointing." Rivka looked at her team. "Shall we head over there and say hi?"

Red nodded.

Ankh walked toward the door. He was ready to go.

"We'll take our leave, Ypsimaximus." Rivka held onto Dery as she bowed. He jumped free and flew back to his mother.

"Thank you, young man, for your clarity of thought." The leader of Ypswich bowed to the boy. Dery waved from the safety of his mom's arms.

Red led the way out.

The group hurried to the escort. "We need a ride to the facilities management building. We have a meeting with Chairman Frenzik."

"I wasn't told about that, but I was told to accommodate you, so that's where we'll go."

Ankh walked around the vehicle on his way back to the ship.

"Why don't you two go with him?" Rivka pointed at Chaz and Dennicron. She didn't want a recording of her activities with Frenzik. She wasn't sure what she was going to do, and she couldn't be sure it would follow protocol.

The two didn't argue. They followed Ankh.

"Just us three," she told the escort. He waited for them to board the shuttle.

"Did you have a good meeting with the Ypsimaximus?"

"We did. Thank you. I think we are agreed on everything we discussed," Rivka offered. She didn't elaborate.

The escort seemed satisfied.

He pointed out architectural highlights as they passed. Rivka grunted her acknowledgments while strangely looking forward to confronting Frenzik and letting him know that he wasn't welcome on Ypswich.

CHAPTER TWENTY-TWO

Facilities Management, Ypswich in the Barrier Nebula

Three Albions walked into the building as the shuttle approached.

Rivka sighed. She wouldn't be waiting for him. She would have to make do. The shuttle stopped, and the door opened. "If you could wait, we'd be obliged," she requested. "We'll handle this from here."

"The Albions have always been kind to me, just so you know."

"Thank you. They have their moments. We'll be back."

Red opened the door and went inside. "Any idea where they might be?" It was a four-story building with multiple wings.

"Any signs?"

In the center of the main floor, they found a building map. Facilities Management was on the top floor

"Going up," Rivka said. They opted for the stairs and climbed quickly.

The door to the office hung open. Red walked in and stepped aside.

The inner office door was also open. Malpace Frenzik walked toward a desk. The other two Albions interposed themselves between Frenzik and the Magistrate.

"Come in, Rivka. We were due another chat, especially after what I just heard from the Ypsimaximus. It appears our contract has been discharged."

Rivka walked in while Red faced off against Frenzik's largest guard. Lindy held Dery close and stayed beside Rivka. Frenzik wouldn't let Rivka get any closer.

"I'm torn up to hear that. I guess you'll be leaving now," Rivka suggested.

"Not quite yet. There might be an opportunity to buy a corporation or three. You see, the Ypsicanti are incredible artists but exceptionally horrible at business." Frenzik picked casually at one of his teeth.

"Predators and their prey, but oddly, I don't have anything to charge you with, and you know how hard I tried to find something. I have no probable cause with which to question you further," Rivka told him.

The two Albion bodyguards held their positions between her and Malpace Frenzik. He was taking no chances regarding a casual brush of the arm or another surreptitious way for Rivka to touch him and see the secrets within his mind.

"These people are begging to be led. That is not a crime. I fill the void, and eventually, I'll govern most aspects of their lives. And they will appreciate it."

"Are you sure?" Rivka angled closer for better eye contact with the chairman.

"I am positive. Otherwise, I wouldn't do it. Governing people is tiring."

"But lucrative," Rivka added.

Frenzik intertwined his fingers across his midsection as he leaned back. "The financial rewards make other things possible, like buying more businesses to further extend Rising Sun's control up and down the supply chain."

"Creating an iron-clad monopoly."

"Eliminating supply chain disruptions. There isn't a dark cloud in every sky, Rivka. Open your eyes and see the sunshine."

"Rising Sun Industries, the sunshine in every day." Rivka clasped her hands behind her back to keep herself from making fists.

"I know you're trying to be facetious, but that is the right way to phrase it. When people want water, it comes without interruption. When they breathe, the air is clean. When they walk down the street, they don't have to worry about their physical safety. Rising Sun is building a single utopia in the Barrier Nebula. You should be thanking me, not vilifying me."

Rivka glared, but Frenzik's eyes sparkled with confidence. He had not and would not rise to the bait. Rivka relaxed. "I should, but I believe history will be your harshest critic, Mr. Frenzik."

"Malpace, Rivka. Say my name. It's okay. Maybe Rising Sun Industries is the model that the rest of the Federation can follow. Business studies will be done on how we manage our business and how we bring peace and prosperity to every culture we touch."

"Peace at a cost. Manufactured chaos. Remove exacerbated friction points. You created the supply chain conditions that drove companies to sell."

"It's all part of business, Rivka. Finding a company's chokepoint and controlling it can lead to better things. You've already found that once I'm in charge of an industry, it flourishes."

It flourished because he choked off supply, but once again, that wasn't illegal. After they sold to Rising Sun, he opened the spigots, and everything flowed once more, raising wages slightly while increasing the workforce. All the while, Rising Sun Industries cashed in, but no one cared because their overall lot in life was improved from the low that Rising Sun had driven it to.

"Moral relativism. Rising Sun shows the workforce how bad it can be before making it better. No matter what, it always looks better, but is it good? Time will tell, Mr. Frenzik."

Rivka held out her hand since it was more of a joke than anything else. He laughed.

"That's not going to happen. Be on your way and keep checking back. You'll find Rising Sun and everything it touches to wear the glitter of gold. We will grow and grow until we can expand beyond the Barrier Nebula. The Federation will find that we're a company to do business with because we deliver. No hard feelings, Rivka. Sometimes, there is no crime."

Frenzik's bodyguard stepped forward and shoved her. Red was there in an instant, forcing himself between the two.

"Watch your mitts, glass jaw," Red warned.

The Albion attempted to push Red, much to Frenzik's

good humor. Red caught his wrist and twisted, gaining leverage with which to shove the Albion guard backward, to stumble against Frenzik's desk.

Rivka knew she should have stopped it, but she needed the satisfaction of a good fight. Red needed it, too. The case had been less than gratifying. She had accomplished little, and for that, she would hold Grainger responsible for giving her a weak case.

Red shrugged off his body armor and cracked his knuckles.

The Albion waited for what he thought was Red's posturing, but it wasn't. Red had been in too many life-or-death fights to take it less than seriously. He sized up his opponent and made sure his body was unrestricted in how he could respond to his bigger opponent.

He feinted and danced, fists up, ready for a regular fight, but the Albion had no intention of fighting that way. He dropped and whipped his leg past, attempting to trip Red. He jumped and cleared the leg, hit the floor, and drove toward the bigger opponent, who was still down on the floor. Red caught him with a heavy fist to the side of the head. The guard's head bounced off the floor before he rolled away and kicked Red off him.

He stood, shaking his head. He crouched like a wrestler. Red stepped forward, offering a knee for a takedown. When the Albion lunged for it, Red rotated it back and followed through with a vicious uppercut that caught his opponent under the chin. The Albion's head snapped back, and his eyes rolled toward the ceiling as he slumped forward and landed face-first on the floor.

"You people never heard of an uppercut?" Red asked

over his unconscious opponent. "As big as you are and no idea how to fight."

Frenzik looked less than amused. He stood and backed against the wall. The other bodyguard positioned himself more tentatively. He raised his fists.

Red took a step toward him.

"That's enough." Rivka held up her hand. "We know you could pummel all three into a coma. We've made our point, and it's time for you to go, too, Frenzik. The Ypswich don't want you here. No one wants you here."

"I want me here," Frenzik countered.

"You'll not get a foothold in Ypswich. I can't fault you for trying because after you get rejected enough times, maybe you'll understand your place."

Rivka nodded once and walked away. Red continued his stare-down of Frenzik's remaining bodyguard before backing away.

They strode briskly out of the office, down the stairs, and outside. The warm air did nothing to improve Rivka's mood.

"Back to my ship, please," she told the escort. She stared out the window, uninterested in small talk. Red and Lindy sat close to her.

She didn't speak during the ride to the ship. She climbed aboard and headed straight for her quarters. Red and Lindy thanked the escort and entered the ship. Dery flew into the airlock, and Red punched the button.

In her quarters, Rivka asked Clevarious to connect her with Grainger.

He answered while she was hunched forward, staring at her hands.

"I guess you didn't decapitate the Hydra."

She looked up. "Dragon. The problem with a Hydra is every head you cut off, it sprouts more heads. And that's this guy. I can't touch him, either literally or figuratively. He's a narcissist, drunk on his own power in a way that can never be sated, but he's going about it incrementally. One company at a time, even though he's spread across the entirety of the Barrier Nebula. Lewbamar and Ypswich are free of Rising Sun's influence. Maybe the others will follow, but there has to be pain first. Right now, all they have is pleasure because none of these people seem particularly well-suited to governing themselves. He offers stability."

"Stability at what cost?"

"He's in charge, and that's incontrovertible."

"What does he do once he's in charge?"

"Lead them to prosperity," Rivka admitted. "I see where he restricts rights through curfews and other controls. It's the slippery slope, but it makes sense. If there's a problem between two and four in the morning, he shuts it down. Problem is moved to where it can better be managed. He controls the supply chain. He improves efficiency. It's hard to appreciate because he's such an arrogant prick."

"Just because he's a prick doesn't mean he's a criminal. Consider this case closed, Rivka. Pack it up and move on. I need you to take the Singularity to Morbius Minor. There's something you have to see.

"The Singularity? What's the issue?"

"It's an issue of succession. You'll figure it out when you get there."

"Estate planning and family law? Come on, Grainger. I

need to punch someone in the face after this case. Maybe a firm knee to the groin. Then I can watch Red beat them senseless. Give me a criminal, a bad one!"

Grainger laughed, but he shook his head. "Wait until you get to Morbius Minor. I think you'll get everything you want and then some."

"Adjudicating an estate. By all the gods, Grainger, if I didn't know better, I'd say you were punishing me."

THE END

JUDGE, JURY, & EXECUTIONER, BOOK 15

If you liked this book, please leave a review. I love reviews since they tell other readers that this book is worth their time and money. I hope you feel that way now that you've finished the latest installment. Please drop me a line and let me know you like Rivka's adventures and want them to continue. This is my new favorite series. I hope you agree.

Don't stop now! Keep turning the pages as Craig hits his *Author Notes* with thoughts about this book and the good stuff that happens in the *Kurtherian Gambit* Universe.

Your favorite legal eagle will return in JJE16, *Succession*!

AUTHOR NOTES - CRAIG MARTELLE

WRITTEN MARCH 2022

Thank you for reading all the way to the end. You are my absolute favorite!

This winter in Fairbanks has been exceptionally harsh. We've had more snow than we've ever had. Temperatures get above freezing every day now. The roads are clear. Spring is coming, finally, and even a little early for us.

I was able to jam this book while sick with some crud, but that led to a serious lung flush, and now I'm breathing better than I have all winter. It's refreshing, although the being sick part sucked. We're going to have a swamp as this mountain of snow melts. It's the same every year. We can hope for a slow melt for the runoff to keep itself under control. We call that breakup. It's when the ice covering the rivers breaks apart and heads downstream.

That's when you stay the hell away from the rivers and

creeks. People die every year getting caught in the ice-choked rapids.

Back to Rivka. I was compelled to write a story where actions that are less than ethical might not rise to the point of being a crime because that's the world we live in now. I want everyone to believe that they can positively effect change to a better way by rejecting those who use a business guillotine to force people to do things that are less than optimal. It's the Tennessee Williams song about the company store. This is that song brought to life in the twenty-third century.

Lots of legalities to explore in this one. I hope it wasn't too much. Not a lot of running and bleeding here, either. Just a touch. JJE16, *Succession* is going to be a good ol' murder mystery with a twist. I like it already, and I hope you do, too. It'll be all the action you expect from Rivka and her team.

Until then, lots of stories to tell. Lots of characters to bring to life.

Peace, fellow humans.

Please join my newsletter (craigmartelle.com—please, please, please sign up!), or you can follow me on Facebook.

If you liked this story, you might like some of my other books. You can join my mailing list by dropping by my website craigmartelle.com, or if you have any comments, shoot me a note at craig@craigmartelle.com. I am always happy to hear from people who've read my work. I try to answer every email I receive.

If you liked the story, please write a short review for me on Amazon. I greatly appreciate any kind words; even one or two sentences go a long way. The number of reviews an eBook receives greatly improves how well an eBook does on Amazon.

Amazon—https://www.amazon.com/author/craigmartelle

BookBub—https://www.bookbub.com/authors/craig-martelle

Facebook—www.facebook.com/authorcraigmartelle

In case you missed it before, my web page—https://craigmartelle.com

That's it. Break's over, back to writing the next book.

OTHER SERIES BY CRAIG MARTELLE

 # - available in audio, too

Terry Henry Walton Chronicles (#) (co-written with Michael Anderle)—a post-apocalyptic paranormal adventure

Gateway to the Universe (#) (co-written with Justin Sloan & Michael Anderle)—this book transitions the characters from the Terry Henry Walton Chronicles to the Bad Company

The Bad Company (#) (co-written with Michael Anderle)—a military science fiction space opera

Judge, Jury, & Executioner (#)—a space opera adventure legal thriller

Shadow Vanguard—a Tom Dublin space adventure series

Superdreadnought (#)—an AI military space opera

Metal Legion (#)—a military space opera

The Free Trader (#)—a young adult science fiction action-adventure

Cygnus Space Opera (#)—a young adult space opera (set in the Free Trader universe)

Darklanding (#) (co-written with Scott Moon)—a space western

Mystically Engineered (co-written with Valerie Emerson)—mystics, dragons, & spaceships

Metamorphosis Alpha—stories from the world's first science fiction RPG

The Expanding Universe—science fiction anthologies

Krimson Empire (co-written with Julia Huni)—a galactic race for justice

Zenophobia (#) (co-written with Brad Torgersen)—a space archaeological adventure

Battleship Leviathan (#)– a military sci-fi spectacle published by Aethon Books

Glory (co-written with Ira Heinichen)—hard-hitting military sci-fi

Black Heart of the Dragon God (co-written with Jean Rabe)—a sword & sorcery novel

End Times Alaska (#)—a post-apocalyptic survivalist adventure published by Permuted Press

Nightwalker (a Frank Roderus series)—A post-apocalyptic western adventure

End Days (#) (co-written with E.E. Isherwood)—a post-apocalyptic adventure

Successful Indie Author (#)—a nonfiction series to help self-published authors

Monster Case Files (co-written with Kathryn Hearst)—A Warner twins mystery adventure

Rick Banik (#)—Spy & terrorism action adventure

Ian Bragg Thrillers (#)—a hitman with a conscience

Not Enough (co-written with Eden Wolfe)—A coming of age contemporary fantasy

Published exclusively by Craig Martelle, Inc

<u>**The Dragon's Call**</u> by Angelique Anderson & Craig A. Price, Jr.—
an epic fantasy quest

<u>**A Couples Travels**</u>—a nonfiction travel series

<u>**Love-Haight Case Files**</u> by Jean Rabe & Donald J. Bingle—the
dead/undead have rights, too, a supernatural legal thriller

<u>**Mischief Maker**</u> by Bruce Nesmith—the creator of Elder Scrolls
V: Skyrim brings you Loki in the modern day, staying true to
Norse Mythology (not a superhero version)

<u>**Mark of the Assassins**</u> by Landri Johnson—a coming of age
fantasy.

For a complete list of Craig's books, stop by his website
—https://craigmartelle.com

BOOKS BY MICHAEL ANDERLE

Sign up for the LMBPN email list to be notified of new releases and special deals!

https://lmbpn.com/email/

For a complete list of books by Michael Anderle, please visit:

www.lmbpn.com/ma-books/